R A Johansen '28

THOSE IN THE CAR WERE TAKEN OFF IN THE BOATS.

Tom Swift and His Airline Express. *Page* 129

TOM SWIFT AND HIS AIRLINE EXPRESS

OR

From Ocean to Ocean by Daylight

By

VICTOR APPLETON

Author of
"Tom Swift and His Motor Cycle"
"Tom Swift Among the Diamond Makers"
"Tom Swift and His Chest of Secrets"
"The Don Sturdy Series"
Etc.

ILLUSTRATED

NEW YORK
GROSSET & DUNLAP
PUBLISHERS

BOOKS FOR BOYS

By VICTOR APPLETON

12mo. Cloth. Illustrated

THE TOM SWIFT SERIES

THE DON STURDY SERIES

GROSSET & DUNLAP, Publishers, New York

CONTENTS

CONTENTS

TOM SWIFT AND HIS AIRLINE EXPRESS

CHAPTER I

SOMETHING QUEER

"Ours is sure a great plant!" murmured Tom Swift to himself, with justifiable pride. "It would be a credit to anybody. No wonder dad loves it, and so do I. Yes, it sure is a great plant! We've had our troubles—our ups and downs—and our enemies have tried their hardest to wipe it out."

Darkness was slowly gathering over the landscape, shrouding in velvety black the trees which were faintly stirring in the summer breeze. Tom, following an old-time cowpath across the green meadow on his way home from town, topped a little rise and caught a glimpse of the high board fence surrounding the Swift Construction Company's plant which he and his father had built up after many years of hard work.

Tom paused for a moment to trace, in the fast-gathering shadows of the night, the outlines of the various buildings—the foundry, the wood-working mill, the electrical shop, the hangars where many types of aircraft were housed.

From some of the tall chimneys faint clouds of smoke arose, for certain of the industries carried on by the Swift Construction Company required that furnaces be kept going day and night.

"A great plant—a wonderful plant!" mused Tom. It gave him a certain sense of pleasure to dwell thus in introspection on the accomplishments of his father and himself. And it buoyed him up for the work in prospect—for Tom Swift had a great plan in mind, a plan so great and daring that, as yet, he had said but little of it even to his father or to Ned Newton, his old chum who was now an officer of the concern.

"But it can be done! I know it can be done!" declared Tom. "And I'm going to do it! I'm going to——"

In his mental energy he had unconsciously spoken the last words in a low voice, but the sight of something just ahead of him in the gathering darkness caused him to break off abruptly and halt suddenly. Concentrating his gaze, Tom Swift looked eagerly at a clump of bushes.

"It's a man," murmured Tom Swift. "A man, sure enough, and it isn't one of our workers, either. None of them would sneak around as he is doing."

For that described exactly the movements of the stranger of whom Tom had caught sight in the darkness as he approached the big fence which surrounded his plant.

"What's he up to?" mused Tom. "No good, that's sure. He wouldn't sneak along like that if he were on the level."

Through Tom's mind flashed remembrances of times when attempts had been made by enemies of himself and his father to fire the plant. To prevent this, and to keep strangers away, a high fence had been erected around the buildings. This fence was protected by wires on the plan of a burglar alarm, so that, no matter at what point the barrier was climbed, a bell would ring in the main office and on an indicator would appear a number to show at what part of the fence an attempt was being made to scale it.

An effort to break down the barrier, or burrow beneath it, would also sound the alarm in like manner. So Tom had no fear that the sneaking stranger, crouching along in the darkness, could get into the midst of the buildings without notice being given.

"But what's his game?" thought Tom.

Almost at the instant he asked himself this question he saw the man crawl behind a clump of bushes. In the natural course of events the man should have appeared on the other side of the clump. But he did nothing of the sort.

"He may be hiding there," mused Tom. "Perhaps waiting for a confederate. I'll just have a closer look at this!"

He advanced boldly toward the bushes. There was nothing between him and the shrubbery, and it was still light enough to see fairly well. Besides, Tom had extraordinarily good eyes. His astonishment can be imagined when, on reaching the bush off which he had not taken his gaze and behind which he had seen the crawling man disappear he found—no one!

"That's the queerest thing I've seen yet!" exclaimed Tom, rubbing his organs of vision.

Standing beside the bush which came about to his shoulders, Tom looked on all sides of it. There was no hollow in the ground, as far as he could make out, no depression and no other clumps of shrubbery and no boulders behind which a man might be hidden. Some distance away there were all of these things in profusion, for the land was wild and uncultivated outside the plant fence. But there was not a hole, boulder, or bush near enough to the one beside which Tom stood to have enabled a man to gain their protection while the young inventor was watching.

"He just crawled back of his bush and then vanished!" said Tom, in a half whisper to himself. "If only I had a flashlight now——" He was startled by hearing someone walking toward him out of the darkness which was now quite dense. "Here he comes!" thought Tom. "Appearing as queerly as he disappeared. Or else it's one of his confederates." He could see no one, and his hand clutched something in his pocket that might be used in case he was attacked.

But a moment later, just as Tom's nerves and muscles were getting tense in anticipation of a struggle, a cheery whistle broke out in the darkness, mingling with the now louder sounds of the footsteps, and Tom, with a cry of relief, called:

"That you, Ned?"

"Sure, old scout!" was the reply. "Oh, there you are!" went on Ned Newton, as he caught sight of Tom at the same moment the young inventor glimpsed his friend and financial manager.

"You're a bit late," went on Ned. "I waited

for you, and when you didn't show up I thought I might as well walk in toward town and maybe I'd meet you."

"Yes, I couldn't get just what I wanted until I had tried two or three places," Tom answered. "And then I met a man——"

Ned broke into a laugh.

"What's the idea?" Tom wanted to know.

"Tell that to Mary!" advised his chum. "She may believe that and then you can tell her another."

"Whew!" shrilly whistled Tom. "I forgot all about Mary. I promised to call on her to-night."

"Sure you did," laughed Ned. "And I've got a date with Helen. You said we'd go over together and——"

"Clean forgot it!" broke in Tom. "And I can't go now. I've got something to do." Quickly he made up his mind to say nothing to Ned of what he had seen until he investigated a little on his own account. "Here, I tell you what to do," went on Tom. "Go on, keep your date with Helen, but when you get to her house telephone to Mary for me and say I'll be a little late. Will you?"

"Pull your chestnuts out of the fire? Is that it, Tom? I reminded you myself before supper!" laughed Ned. "Well, I don't mind, for you've done the same for me. I guess Mary Nestor knows you by this time, or, if she doesn't, she never will. But what's the big idea?"

"Oh, I've just got a notion in my head," said Tom. "I want to go to the office a moment to jot down some memoranda before I forget them. 'Phone Mary I'll be over as soon as I can. See you later."

"Cheek!" exclaimed Ned, and with his merry whistle he hurried off in the darkness. "I only hope Mary speaks to you when you finally get to see her," floated back to Tom.

"Don't you worry about Mary," advised the young inventor. "I'll explain to her. And tell her I'll be along in about half an hour. I really forgot all about the engagement."

"I'll say you did!" playfully mocked Ned.

Then, with his chum out of the way, Tom gave himself to trying to solve the mystery. For mystery he believed it to be. Seeing a man step behind a bush and, on arriving at the bush, to find nothing of the man there was surprising, to say the least.

Sensing that it would soon be so dark that it would be useless to investigate without an illuminant of some sort, Tom made haste to gain what advantage he could from the fast-fading light. He looked sharply about without moving from his place behind the bush on the other side of which he had seen the man disappear. Then, as he could pick up here no clew to the strange happening, the young inventor moved around to the other side.

The light was a little better here and Tom saw something that made him fairly gasp with astonishment. He had moved somewhat away from the bush and almost at his feet was an opening in the ground.

"This explains it!" murmured Tom, half aloud. "A hole in the ground! He went down there. I knew he couldn't have dug himself in as quickly as that. But that hole! I never saw it before. It isn't any of our doing. I'd have known about it if it were."

All the land there belonged to Tom and his father. It was a big field surrounding the fenced-in plant, and often the smooth part of the field was used as a landing place for aeroplanes.

Cautiously approaching the opening in the ground and wondering more and more how it had gotten there without his knowledge, Tom saw that it had been closed by some planks placed over it. These were now tossed to one side, as if they had been hurriedly displaced. Scattered about was loose earth which had evidently covered the planks, thus hiding them from the view of a casual observer.

"A secret opening!" murmured Tom. "This is certainly the queerest thing I've ever seen! What does it mean?"

His surprise increased when, as he drew near to the edge of the opening, he saw a rough flight of plank steps going down into the hole. The young man caught his breath sharply, it was so astounding. But with Tom Swift to see and think was to act, and a moment later he began a descent of the steps into the mysterious hole. It might have been the part of discretion to wait until daylight, but a secret opening like this, so near the Swift plant, could mean but one thing, Tom reasoned.

"Some one is trying to put up a game on us," he decided. "Unknown to us he has made a tunnel under our plant. There's something funny here! I'm going to see what it is."

Tom had fairly to feel his way down the flight of plank steps. They were rough and uneven, but solidly built. The young inventor counted them as he descended so he would know how to come back. Now that his head was below the level of the ground it was so dark that it was as if a velvet robe had been wrapped about him.

He counted ten steps down, and was cautiously feeling about with his right foot extended to ascertain if there were any more, when suddenly he felt the presence of some one near him. He caught the sound of breath fiercely drawn in, as if his unknown and unseen companion, there in the darkness, was nerving himself for an attack.

Instinctively Tom drew back, his hands pressed to the planked sides of the opening down which he had descended. He could feel, rather than see, some one leaning toward him. A sweet, sickening odor came to his nostrils. He felt a hand pressed over his face—a hand that held a damp rag which gave off that overpowering perfume.

"Here! What's this? Who—who——" But Tom Swift's voice became a mere gurgle in his throat. His legs became limp. His head whirled and he seemed lifted up and carried through measureless miles of space on the wings of some great bird.

Then Tom's senses left him. He knew no more.

CHAPTER II

WAITING IN THE DARK

JUST how long Tom Swift remained unconscious he himself did not know. It may have been several hours, for when he came to himself he felt a curious stiffness about his muscles as if he had lain for some time on the damp ground.

And he was on the ground—a fact he ascertained by feeling about with his hands, his fingers encountering damp, packed earth and the smooth surface of stones set in the soil.

"Where in the world am I, and what happened?" thought Tom, as soon as he could collect his senses enough to do any thinking. "Gee, but I sure do feel queer!"

There was a sickish taste in his mouth—a sense of sweetness, such as he remembered followed a slight operation he had undergone some years before when an anæsthetic had been given him.

"They doped me all right—that's what they

did," mused Tom. "Ether, chloroform, or something like that. It knocked me out. But I'm beginning to feel all right again—no headache or anything like that. But what does it all mean, and where am I?"

Those were questions not easily answered.

While Tom Swift is trying to collect his senses and to remember, in their sequence, the events which led up to his queer predicament, may I take just a moment of your time, if you are a new reader, to tell you who Tom was?

The first book of this series, "Tom Swift and His Motor Cycle," introduces you to the young inventor. His father, Barton Swift, was a widower, living in the old homestead at Shopton on Lake Carlopa. The Swift home was on the outskirts of the town and in a building not far from the house Barton Swift began work on a series of inventions which were destined to make him and his son famous. Tom's mother was dead, but Mrs. Baggert, the housekeeper, looked well after the material welfare of Tom and his father.

In due time Tom began to follow in his father's footsteps, working at small inventions until, when a sturdy youth, he became possessed of a motorcycle. He bought the machine of an eccentric individual named Wakefield Damon, who lived in the neighboring town of Waterfield. Mr. Damon set out to learn to ride his new machine.

"But bless my porous plaster!" the queer man would exclaim in telling the story, "I never thought the contraption was going to climb trees!"

Which it did, or tried to, because Mr. Damon did not know how to manage it. The result was that the rider was injured and the motorcycle badly smashed and Tom, near whose home the accident occurred, became the owner of the machine.

How he repaired it, added some improvements, and what he did with the machine are fully set forth in the book. It was the beginning of a long friendship with Mr. Damon, and also the real start of Tom's inventive career.

Those of you who have followed him in his successes, from his motor boat to "Tom Swift's Chest of Secrets,"—the volume immediately preceding this one—need not be told of Tom's activities. He had made some wonderful pieces of apparatus and had had some startling adventures. In some of these his father and Mr. Damon had shared. So, also, had Ned Newton, Tom's closest friend and now the treasurer of the Swift Construction Company.

Mary Nestor, of whom Ned had spoken, was a beautiful girl whom Tom hoped to marry some day, and Ned Newton was interested in a similar manner in Mary's friend, Helen Morton.

As Tom sat there in the darkness, trying to puzzle out where he was and how he had gotten there, his thought flashed to Mary.

"I wonder what she'll think?" he mused. "I'd better get to a telephone and explain. Let's see. I was coming back from town and I saw some fellow sneaking along behind the bushes. I met Ned. I went down a flight of stairs in a hole—though how they could be there and I not know it, is more than I can fathom. Then they doped me. But who did it and why, I don't know. I'll soon find out, though. Wonder how long I've been here? Feels like a week, I'm so stiff. But I'm not hurt, thank goodness!"

Tom stretched out his arms in the darkness. They responded to the action of his muscles. But when he tried to get up and walk—well, he simply could not!

"Chained fast!" cried Tom, aloud. His hands had sought his left ankle when he found that something held him fast there, and his fingers had come in contact with a chain.

For a moment he felt a sinking sensation. To be chained fast in the dark, at the bottom of some cave or dungeon, located he knew not where, was enough to take the heart out of any one. But not for long did Tom Swift give way to despair.

He gave a vigorous tug to the chain about his ankle. After all, it might only be lying across it or loosely twisted. But it needed only one effort on his part to loosen the links to let him know that he was bound fast. Whoever had put the chain on his ankle had done so with serious intentions of holding the young inventor captive.

"Well, this is worse and more of it!" he mused grimly. "What does it all mean? It can't be a plot to kidnap me. No one knew I was coming across the lots, for I didn't know it myself until the last minute. And seeing that man sneaking along, discovering the secret stairs— it was all a series of accidents. Though it's likely to prove a serious accident for me if I can't get loose."

Tom was nothing if not practical, and first he felt about with his hands to determine the exact nature of what it was that held him fast. He discovered, by the sense of touch, that something in the nature of a handcuff was snapped about his ankle. To this cuff, or leg-iron, was attached a chain. By following this, link by link, Tom found that the chain was made fast to a ring of iron which, in turn, was sunk into the stone side wall of the cave or tunnel in which he now found himself.

How far he was removed from the bottom of the flight of secret steps where he had been made unconscious, he did not know, any more than he knew where he was.

Having discovered what it was that held him fast and the nature of the chain and its fastenings, Tom, who had risen to his feet, stood silent a moment, listening. It was very black and very still in the cave, if such it was, and from the earthy, damp smell he concluded that he must be underground, or at least in some vault or cellar.

By test Tom found that he could move about five feet, such being the length of the chain. The leg-iron had been snapped or riveted about his ankle outside of his trousers. It was not tight enough to cause any pain, but it was snug enough to be impossible of removal.

"They've got me as tight as an animal in a trap!" grimly exclaimed the youth, when, by a series of tugs, he ascertained how securely the end of the chain was fast in the rocky wall. "Just like a trap, or a prisoner in an old-time dungeon!" bitterly reflected the young man. "All it needs to make a moving picture film is some beautiful maiden to come to my rescue with a file——"

Tom's spoken words (for he was talking aloud to himself) came to a sudden end as he clapped a hand to the pocket of his coat.

"I've got 'em!" he fairly shouted, and he drew out a small paper parcel in which were two keen files. They were part of the purchases made just before stumbling on the mysterious man and finding the steps in the queer opening.

"Files—the hardest and best made!" he told himself. "They'll cut through anything but a diamond. Luck's with me, after all. They didn't know I had these! Oh, boy!"

Everything seemed changed now! Though he was held fast, though he was in some secret dungeon, hope sang a song of joy in his heart.

For a moment Tom debated with himself as to the best end of the chain at which to begin filing. It would be more comfortable with that leg-iron off his ankle, but by feeling it in the darkness he could tell that it was broad and thick. It would take some time for even the keen, hard file to cut through it.

"I'll file through one of the links close to the leg-iron," decided Tom. "That won't leave much to carry around, and it won't take long to cut through a link—that is, unless they're made of case-hardened steel."

But the chain was of the ordinary sort, made of soft iron, and it did not take the young inventor long, practiced as he was in the use of tools, to file apart one of the links. True it was not easy in the darkness, and, more than once, the file slipped and cut Tom's hands or fingers, for he changed from left to right and back to left in using the file, having taught himself to be ambidextrous in many operations.

At last he could feel that the link was nearly severed and then, inserting the small ends of the two files in it, he pried them apart. This leverage broke the thin remaining bit of iron and Tom was free.

That is, he was free to move about as he pleased, but he was still within the dark cave, and where it was he could not imagine.

"I've got to feel my way about," he told himself. "It's as dark as the inside of a pocket."

So dark was it that Tom had to tread cautiously and with outstretched hands lest he bump into some obstruction. Whether he was moving toward the steps down which he had come or in the opposite direction, Tom had no means of knowing. His sense of touch alone guided him.

He could feel that he was walking along a tunnel, but the size of it he could only guess at. Then, suddenly, on making an elbow turn, he saw, glimmering in the distance, a faint light. It was the light of day, Tom knew, and by that

he realized that he had been held captive all
night.

"That makes it bad," he mused. "Dad will
have done a lot of worrying about me, I'm
afraid. But I guess I'll soon be out of here."

Then, to his ears, came the murmur of voices
—voices strange to him. So faint was the light
in the distance that it was of no service to him
where he stood waiting in the darkness; waiting
for he knew not what.

The voices increased in loudness, showing that
the speakers were approaching. Then he heard
footsteps echoing strangely in the hollow tunnel.

"If there's going to be a fight I'd better get
ready for it," Tom told himself fiercely. He
stooped and began feeling about on the ground
for a loose rock or a club. But he could find
nothing. Then like a flash it came to him.

"One of the files! They're pretty sharp on
the handle end. As good as a knife! I'll use it
like a knife if I have to," he mused desperately.

He drew one of the files from his pocket,
grasped it firmly, and waited in the darkness
for what was to happen next.

CHAPTER III

MASKED MEN

AFTER the treatment that had been accorded him, Tom Swift rather welcomed than otherwise a chance to come to grips with the men who were responsible for his position. Usually even-tempered and generous, just now he felt eager for vengeance and he would not have cared much if two men had attacked him at once.

Strangely enough he did not feel weak or ill now. He had, somewhat, when he first regained his senses after having been overpowered by some drug. But his brain had cleared and he kept himself in such good physical trim all the while that even a night of unconsciousness had not sapped his strength.

The light in the distance did not increase any, from which Tom gathered that it was full daylight with the sun well above the horizon, and after that first murmur of voices and the sound of footsteps these sounds did not come any nearer. Nor did Tom catch a glimpse of any figures between himself and that little circle of light.

Then from some point outside the cave or tunnel he heard voices calling. They were louder than the first, and there seemed to be some dispute or disturbance.

The voices rose to a high pitch and then died away. Silence followed, and then came the sound of retreating footsteps.

"They're going away!" exulted Tom. "Now I've got a chance to walk toward that daylight and see where I am. Maybe I'd better wait a few minutes, though. They may come back."

He waited what he thought was several minutes and then, hearing no other sounds of voices or footsteps, began a cautious approach toward that gleam of light. What a blessed thing light was, after all that black and clinging darkness!

In silence Tom crept on, advancing one foot after the other cautiously, and keeping one hand extended to give warning of his approach toward any obstruction while in his other hand he held the file like a dagger, ready to use.

But there was no occasion for this. A little later he found himself standing in a circle of daylight illumination that filtered down an inclined shaft which led out of a tunnel, such as

Tom could now ascertain he was in. A natural tunnel it appeared to be, with rocks jutting out here and there in the earthen sides. Roughly the tunnel was in the form of a half circle, the floor being flat and the roof arched. The inclined entrance led upward in a gentle slope.

"Well, now to see what's up there!" said Tom to himself, taking a long breath and holding his weapon ready. He tensed his muscles and steeled his nerves for what he felt might be a desperate struggle. Yet he did not shrink back.

As he advanced cautiously, step by step, up the incline that led to daylight and the outer world, he felt at first a sense of disappointment when he saw no one with whom he might come to grips. He had been treated so meanly that it would have been a source of satisfaction to have had it out in a rough-and-tumble fight with those responsible.

But, to his surprise, Tom pushed his way out through a tangle of underbrush and bushes which grew about this end of the tunnel and found none to dispute him. This surprise was added to when he looked about him and found out where he was.

"On Barn Door Island!" exclaimed Tom. "Of all places! Barn Door Island! But how did I get here? It's miles away from where I went down those steps near our plant. Of all places! Barn Door Island!"

This was a small island in Lake Carlopa which had been named Barn Door because, some time or other, one of the early settlers happened to remark that it was no larger than the door of a barn. The island was at the end of the lake farthest removed from Shopton and the Swift plant.

"I never knew there was an entrance to a tunnel here!" said Tom, as he looked about him. "But then I've never explored here very much."

Nor had any of the other lads of Shopton. Barn Door Island was a barren place—merely a collection of scrubby trees and tangled bushes and great boulders set down at the swampy end of Lake Carlopa. It was not a good fishing location and too dreary for picnic parties, so Barn Door was seldom visited.

"But if I had an idea there was a tunnel entrance here—the beginning of a passage that led under the lake and under the land right up to our place I'd have done a lot of exploring, that's sure!" Tom told himself. "That's a natural tunnel, I'm positive of it, at least most of it is. Somebody went along it until they got to the end near our fence. Then they broke out, put in those steps and made the plank covering for the opening. They put earth over the planks so no one would see them. That part must have been done recently, for we were trying airships out in that field a month ago and I landed right near that bush behind which the man disappeared. I know I did, for I remember thinking I might crash into the fence. So the land end of this queer tunnel has only been opened lately. This island end must have been here a long while. But it's queer no one knew of it. And I wonder what it's being used for? Something to do with our business, I'm sure. Our enemies are at work again!"

Tom quickly reviewed the situation in his mind. Since his Chest of Secrets had been taken and he had had so much trouble in recovering it, he had been very cautious about his plans of new inventions. Suspecting several of his newer employes, he had gotten rid of them and had taken great precautions, on the advice of Ned and his father.

"But if there's a tunnel from this lonely island under the lake and beneath the shore right up almost to our plant, it means that something desperate is in the wind," reasoned Tom. "They must have resented my blundering into it as I did, and they tried to put me out of the way. After they doped me they must have carried me a long way through the tunnel, to chain me fast near this end.

"Well, I'm free now, and out in the open. About noon, I should judge by the sun and by the way my stomach feels," Tom went on, with a grim smile, for he was getting hungry and feeling a bit weak now. "I hope it isn't more than the next day," he went on, meaning the day following his night encounter with Ned.

He looked about him. Barn Door Island was about five acres in extent, large enough, on account of its wild character, to give concealment to any number of enemies. But if there were any such here now they did not show themselves as Tom eagerly and anxiously scanned the somewhat wild landscape.

"Well, now that I know where I am, though I can't understand how or why I was put in that tunnel and chained," mused the lad, as he looked at the iron still on his leg, "I might as well try to get back home. It's pretty lonesome down here, and I don't know whether I can signal any one or not. But it isn't far to the mainland and I can swim it. Though if I'm going to do that I'd better file this iron off. No fun swimming with that bracelet on my ankle."

He looked about for a place where he could sit down and file in comfort at the remaining evidence of his recent bondage when, as he approached the shore, he saw, pulled up close to a rude dock in a little cove, a small motor boat.

"Well, if this isn't luck!" cried Tom. "There must be some picnic party here and that's their boat. But no—wait a minute! Maybe it belongs to those men I heard talking in the tunnel. I'll wager that's it. And this is my chance! I'll appropriate their boat since they treated me like a roughneck. I'll get back home, maybe in time to stop their trick—whatever it is."

There was not much about a motor boat that Tom Swift did not know, and it took him but a few seconds to ascertain that this one was in good working order. No longer considering the need of filing off the leg-iron, Tom pushed the boat out from the dock, which was merely a few old logs and planks, and prepared to start the engine.

He turned the flywheel and, almost at the first revolution after he had thrown the spark switch, the engine was in motion. But even as it glided out of the little cove Tom was aware of the presence of another craft. Around one of the points of the cove, as he guided his boat out, the other swung in, and a glance showed it to be occupied by four rough-looking men.

Two of them wore masks. The faces of the other two were familiar to Tom, for they were two of his recently discharged workmen— Kenny and Schlump!

Tom had a feeling that some desperate work was in prospect. The attack on him, the rendering of him unconscious, his being chained fast—all this was more than accidental coincidence following his trailing of the man who had disappeared down in the tunnel.

For a moment those in the second boat remained gazing, spellbound, it seemed, at Tom, who was rapidly putting distance between himself and those he felt were his enemies. The boat he had so unexpectedly found proved to be a speedy little craft. But the other was also.

"There's Tom Swift now!" cried Schlump, pointing.

"Where?" asked one of the masked men.

"In our boat!" Schlump answered. "Come back here!" he roared, shaking his fist at Tom.

"Come back nothing!" taunted the young inventor.

"Don't stop to talk!" shouted one of the masked men. "Speed up! We must catch Swift at any cost!"

CHAPTER IV

A NIGHT OF WORRY

ABOUT nine o'clock on the night when Tom
Swift had witnessed the strange actions of the
man who so mysteriously disappeared, the telephone bell tinkled in the Swift home. As Tom's
father was reading a scientific book in which he
was much engrossed, Mrs. Baggert went to the
instrument. Half-interested in the conversation, Mr. Swift listened to the one-sided talk,
hearing Mrs. Baggert say:

"Oh, how do you do, Miss Nestor? No, Tom
isn't here. I haven't seen him since supper.
His father is here. Do you want to speak to
him? What's that? Oh, all right. Yes, I'll
be sure to tell him."

"Isn't Tom over at Mary's house?" asked
the aged inventor, with a shade of anxiety in his
voice as he looked up from his book. He had
guessed at what he had not heard.

"No, he isn't there, and Miss Nestor is getting
tired of waiting, I guess," answered the housekeeper.

"Where is Tom?" asked his father.

"I don't know," Mrs. Baggert replied. "He started for Shopton right after supper, saying he had to buy some things at the hardware store before it closed. I heard Mr. Ned tell him not to be late and Tom promised he wouldn't. I didn't know then what Mr. Ned warned him not to be late for, but I can guess now that it was in calling on Miss Nestor."

"And he hasn't arrived there yet," murmured Mr. Swift. "That's a bit odd, for Tom doesn't usually break his engagements—especially with Mary Nestor," and he smiled a little.

"Oh, Miss Nestor told me to say to you that she wasn't in the least worried," Mrs. Baggert made haste to add. "She says she knows Tom is very busy and something may have come up at the last moment. She says he promised to take her to see a moving picture this evening. She has been waiting some time, and she called up to say if he couldn't come it would be all right, and she would go to the second show with her mother. That's all the message was about."

"Oh, well, I guess it's all right then," returned Mr. Swift, with an air of relief. "Tom is prob-ably delayed in Shopton, getting what he wanted. But he should have telephoned, either here or to Mary. It isn't fair to keep a young lady waiting like that."

"Miss Nestor said to be sure and tell him she wasn't at all put out because he didn't come," said Mrs. Baggert. "She knows it must be some good reason that kept him away."

"I hope it is," said Mr. Swift. "But it isn't like Tom to stay away without sending some word."

As the hours passed and the young inventor neither returned nor communicated, the anxiety in his father's mind grew, until, about midnight when the front door was heard to open, Mr. Swift cried:

"Is that you, Tom? Where have you been? Why didn't you send some word? And you have broken your promise to call on Mary!"

"This isn't Tom," came in the voice of Ned Newton, who, of late, had been living at the Swift home. "But you don't mean to tell me Tom isn't here! I was just going to tell him he was in for a bad half-hour the next time he called on Mary."

"No, Ned, Tom isn't here," said Mr. Swift, who had sat up past his usual retiring hour to meet his son when he should arrive. "And he isn't over at Mary's house, either."

"I know he isn't there," Ned said. "Helen and I stopped in on our way back from the pictures to find out why we hadn't seen those two at the show. We found Mary a bit dis-

turbed because Tom had neither called nor
telephoned. That's why I was going to tell him
he was in for a bad time when next he sees
Mary."

"But he isn't here," said Mr. Swift. "I
can't understand it. He went over to Shopton
directly after supper, Mrs. Baggert says, and he
hasn't returned."

"Oh, yes, he came back," Ned replied quickly.
"I saw him."

"Where?" cried the aged inventor.

"Just outside the big fence—on the landing
field, in fact. Tom was on his way here then.
He found what he wanted in some Shopton
store, he told me, and I said he'd better hurry
if he was going to keep his date with Mary. I
was a bit late myself, so I left him and hurried
on and he started for the house."

"Then something has happened to him, for
he never got here!" exclaimed Mr. Swift.
"Something has happened!" He was getting
excited and Ned did not like that, for the aged
man's health was far from good.

"Oh, not necessarily," said Ned, in easier
tones than his own feelings justified. "Tom's
all right, you can be sure of that. He knows
how to take care of himself. Besides, how
could anything happen at his own doorstep, so
to speak? He was near the big fence."

"Well, I'm sure something has happened," Mr. Swift declared.

But Ned shook his head and smiled.

"More than likely," he said, "Tom went into his private office to leave what he had bought in Shopton. Once he was at his desk he saw something he had forgotten to do, or he was taken with a sudden idea, and he sat down to make some note about it before it slipped out of his mind.

"It isn't the first time he has done that, nor the first time he has made dates with Mary and then forgotten all about them. Don't worry, Mr. Swift, you'll find Tom in his private office over at the works."

"That is easily settled," was the answer. "I'll call him on the telephone."

There was an instrument in the living room where this conversation took place. The Swift home and works were linked by intercommunicating telephones, and Mr. Swift was soon plugging in on the circuit that connected with Tom's private office. While he was waiting Mrs. Baggert came quietly into the room behind Mr. Swift.

"Is Tom home?" she asked of Ned, forming the words with her lips but not speaking, since she did not want to disturb Mr. Swift. Ned shook his head in negation, and a puzzled look spread over the face of the housekeeper.

"They're too easily worried," mused Ned, half-smiling. "Tom is all right, I'm sure."

But this certainty gradually disappeared when several seconds went by and there was no answer to the bell that must be ringing in Tom's office at the works.

"Isn't he there?" Ned could not help asking.

"He doesn't seem to be," Mr. Swift replied.

"Maybe he's on his way home," Ned was saying when Mr. Swift suddenly exclaimed:

"Some one is at the 'phone now! Oh, hello, Koku!" he called into the transmitter. "Yes, I am here. But where's Tom? Is he there? What? He isn't? Has he been there? No!"

The silence on Mr. Swift's part, following his last word, told Ned and Mrs. Baggert, more than anything else, how worried he was. He appeared to be listening to what the giant at the other end of the wire was saying. Then he spoke again:

"We'll be right over, Koku. Yes, I'm coming and so is Mr. Newton. Don't bring Eradicate? Well, he might be of some help. There's no use in you being jealous. Look around until we get there. Tom may be in some of the other buildings!"

Slowly Mr. Swift replaced the receiver on

the hook and then, turning to Ned and the housekeeper, he said:

"Tom isn't there and hasn't been since he left early in the afternoon. Koku has just made his rounds and hasn't seen him, but I told him to go over the place again and have the other watchmen go with him. We'll go ourselves and help search. I'm sure something has happened to Tom!"

CHAPTER V

A CRASH

ADVENTURES in plenty had befallen Tom Swift, and in many of them Ned Newton had had a share. But always the young inventor had come out "on top of the heap," so perhaps Ned was justified in his feeling that everything would be all right. Still he could understand and appreciate Mr. Swift's worry.

Mr. Swift began looking for his hat and neck scarf, this last on the suggestion of his housekeeper.

A little later Mr. Swift, Ned, and Eradicate, the aged colored servant who had been in the Swift family many years, were on their way to the big plant, almost a mile distant. Ned had brought around to the door one of the small cars Tom used to make trips between his home and the shop, and it did not take long to reach the main gate in the big fence surrounding the place.

So many and varied had been the attempts to

rob Tom of the fruits of his and his father's brains that drastic measures to guard the place had been put into effect. The big fence, impossible to scale without long ladders, was one protection. In addition there were burglar alarm wires along the fence, which wires would give warning of any attempt to get under it or over it. In addition there was a strip of metal, charged with a high-power current which could be turned on at will, and this would give unauthorized trespassers a severe shock. It would not kill, but would disable for a time.

In addition there were other forms of protection, and so well guarded were the different gates, by night and day, that not even Tom himself could get in without due formality. So it was when the party of searchers arrived, they were not at once let in. The guard at the gate must first be certain who he was admitting.

"Good lan'!" exclaimed Eradicate. "Dish is plum' foolishness! Cain't yo' look an' see dat ole Massa Swift hisse'f am heah?"

"They have to be cautious, Rad," said Ned, as he got out of the machine to give the password which was used each night. He saw Koku, the giant, coming down the path inside the fence, and the big man at once recognized the visitors.

Between Eradicate and Koku there was

rivalry and jealousy because each one wanted to serve Tom without having the other called on. And no sooner had the colored man caught sight of the giant, as the latter told the watchman to open the gate, than Eradicate burst out with:

"Hu! Dat's jest laik de big ninny! Don't know his own folks! It's a wonder to me dat Massa Tom keep him, he's so dumb!"

"Black man talk much—not do anything!" growled the giant. "Look out or um be squashed," and he opened and closed his enormous hands as if he wanted to clutch the old servant in them.

"That will do now, you two!" warned Mr. Swift. "We came to find Tom. Are you sure he isn't here, Koku?"

"Not too sure, master. Not sure much about Master Tom—he go—he come—no can tell—no can do."

"That's about right," agreed Ned, with a laugh. "Tom certainly goes and comes without telling any one much about it. But I gathered, from what he said to me just outside the fence, that he would be right along. There didn't seem to be anything special he had to do."

"Just where was it you met him?" asked Mr. Swift. "Let us start the investigation from there, you and I, Ned. Meanwhile, I will

have all the other shops called by telephone from the central here."

He gave orders to this effect to one of the watchmen and then with Ned went to the place, outside the fence, where Tom had last talked with his chum. But it was dark, and Ned, naturally, could not point out the exact spot, even with the aid of a flashlight.

"I think it was here, near this rock and bush," he said, throwing the gleam of his little electric torch about.

But the dry, hard ground gave no clews to this superficial examination, and, as a matter of fact, Ned was about twenty-five feet off in his calculations, as was demonstrated later. Otherwise he and Mr. Swift might have seen the hole in the ground and the flight of stairs, for it was not until some time later that night—near morning, as a matter of fact—that the plotters replaced the planks and spread earth over them, thus hiding the secret entrance.

"Well, there doesn't seem to be anything here," said Mr. Swift, with an uneasy sigh as they made a hasty examination of the place. "We had better go inside and look there."

But the search in and about the many buildings of the great Swift plant was no more successful. Every office and shop telephone had been rung. Some were answered by guards

or watchmen who happened to be in the vicinity at the time the bell rang. But one and all said they had not seen Tom.

Then there was a check-up of every gate and entrance in the big fence, and at no place had Tom been admitted. Granting that his protective plans worked, he could not have entered his own plant without a record having been made of it, and there was none.

"There's only one answer to this, then," said Ned, when the search had ended.

"What's the answer?" asked Mr. Swift.

"Tom didn't come in here after he left me. He must have gone somewhere else."

Mr. Swift looked at his watch.

"Do you suppose he could be at Mary's now?" he asked.

"What time is it?"

"Three."

"No, he wouldn't be there at this hour!" declared Ned.

"He might," replied Mr. Swift hopefully. "When Tom's mind is busy on his inventions he forgets all about time. It would be just like him to forget that it was three o'clock in the morning and go to call on Mary."

Ned shook his head, but Mr. Swift went on:

"I'm going to call her presently. But there is just one more place I want to search. It's in

the vault where we keep the Chest of Secrets, as Tom calls it. There is a private entrance to that he could come in by and not register the alarm nor be seen by any of the guards. He can switch off that alarm from his room at the house. I'll look there. He may have gone there to see if there isn't some way out in the trouble we're in over the airline express patents."

"Trouble?" questioned Ned, as they walked toward the vault.

"Yes. Tom and I haven't spoken of it even to you, Ned, for the thing really isn't in such shape that it can be talked about. But Tom has an idea, it may be nothing more than a dream, that he can establish a line of travel to cross our continent from New York to San Francisco between dawn and darkness. In other words, a coast-to-coast service, from ocean to ocean, by daylight—say sixteen hours—with no change."

"No change!" cried Ned. "What's the idea —refueling the planes in the air? Of course that has been done. But from coast to coast in sixteen hours without change! It can't be done!"

"Tom thinks so," said Mr. Swift. "That's what he's working on now. He has had some new models made, but there is trouble over the patent rights. Some one is trying to get his

idea away from him. It may be that Tom came to the secret vault after he left you to make sure everything was all right, and he may be there yet."

But the vault was unoccupied, nor had it been disturbed. Mr. Swift gave a hasty glance at several complicated and odd-looking models of aircraft in the concrete room, looked over a pile of papers, and said:

"Well, they haven't been disturbed since Tom and I were here last, which proves my son hasn't been here. But where is he? I'm beginning to get worried, Ned. More worried than ever!"

"Oh, he'll be all right," was the answer, though in his own heart Ned Newton could not help feeling apprehensive. "It may be, as you say, that he made a very late call on Mary, and her folks have probably asked him to stay all night, as they have done before."

"I think the matter justifies me in calling Mr. Nestor on the telephone," said Mr. Swift, as they emerged from the vault where the Chest of Secrets was stored. "It's rather early to ring up anybody, but I guess they will understand."

It was about four o'clock now, and already, in the east, a light was appearing, the sun was heralding the dawn. The early birds were beginning to sing. It would soon be morning, though not yet time for the wheels to begin humming in the Swift plant.

Going back to the office, where Koku reported that a second check-up had failed to disclose the whereabouts of the young inventor, Mr. Swift called the Shopton central operator and gave her the number of the Nestor house.

There was some little delay, as was natural when a call is made at that hour of the morning, but at length Mr. Nestor's voice was heard.

"Who? Tom? No, he isn't here—hasn't been here," was the message the aged inventor received. "What's the matter?"

There was some further talk, and Mr. Swift briefly oulined what had happened.

"Don't alarm Mary yet," Mr. Swift cautioned his friend. "But I fear something has happened to Tom. I wish you would come over."

"I will!" Mr. Nestor promised. "I'll be over as soon as I can dress."

"Tell him I'll call for him," Ned said to Mr. Swift, and this message went over the wires.

It was fully light when they went down into the yard where the small auto had been left. And suddenly the silence of the dawn, made musical by the twitterings of the birds, was broken by an increasing roar and throbbing noise.

"Airship!" grunted Koku.

"Suah enough!" exclaimed Eradicate, pointing up. "Dere she am!"

The throbbing sound became louder, and a moment later they saw the plane, a large one, approaching from the west.

"It's Mr. Damon's machine!" cried Ned. "What in the world is he flying so early for? He isn't sure enough of himself to take that big plane out alone—he only got it the other day. Great Scott! Look! He's going to hit your mooring mast!"

At one end of the big landing field outside the fence Tom had recently erected a tall steel mast, to which he moored a small dirigible balloon with which he was conducting experiments. As all looked up they saw Mr. Damon in his new machine headed straight for this mast.

"He doesn't know it's there!" cried Ned. "He's sure going to hit!"

A moment later there was an alarming crash, and the top of the mast was seen to break off while one edge of the aeroplane's left wing crumpled.

CHAPTER VI

AGAIN A PRISONER

THE threat which Tom Swift heard the men in the pursuing motor boat mutter—a threat to catch him at any cost—was not needed to cause him to speed up the craft he had appropriated in an endeavor to escape. The sinister character of the men who wore the masks he could easily guess at. As to the others, he had begun to suspect them soon after they obtained work in his plant. Though they were clever mechanics, Tom did not like Kenny and Schlump and so had directed their discharge.

"They either have it in for me on that account," mused Tom, as he made an adjustment to the motor to get more speed, "or else there's something deeper in the plot. I guess they must have chained me up after I blundered into their tunnel. I'd like to know what all this means, but now is not the time to stop and find out. I must get away and ask questions afterward."

It was to be a desperate chase—Tom Swift realized that from the tense and eager manner of the men in the boat now plowing through the waters of Lake Carlopa. They were forcing their craft to her best speed in an endeavor to overtake him.

"It's a wonder they don't begin shooting," mused Tom. "A crowd of men like that, with two of them masked, won't stop at shooting. Maybe I'd better get down a bit."

He had been standing up in the boat, the better to make adjustments to the motor, but now, as he thought of the possibility of being fired upon, he crouched down to give less of a target to the men.

This move of his seemed to be misinterpreted by the pursuers, for one of them cried:

"There he goes overboard! One of you take after him!" This was shouted by one of the masked men, whose identity Tom Swift could only guess at, though he judged all of them to be some of his enemies.

But the young inventor had no intention of jumping out of the boat to swim for safety. He knew he would soon be overtaken and captured. His only chance lay in beating the scoundrels in a race. Besides, he was in no physical condition to endure a long swim. He had been in a most uncomfortable, cramped position all night, and the exertion of filing off the chain and going through the tunnel to emerge on Barn Door Island had tired him. He had had no breakfast, and this lack was now beginning to make itself felt more than at first.

But as he crouched down in the boat, where only a small part of his body showed above the rail, he remembered that he had in his pocket some chocolate candy. He had bought it the night before on his trip to town.

"I'll make a breakfast on that," mused Tom. So as he crouched there in the boat he reached into his pocket, got out the cake of chocolate, and began to nibble it. In a few minutes he felt decidedly better. That "gone" feeling had left his stomach, and he began to relish, rather than fear, the outcome of the impending struggle.

The pursuit had started at the end of the lake where there was no town or other settlement, but at the pace it would not be more than half an hour before he would sight his home town.

For a few moments after the wild chase began Tom could hear the men in the other boat shouting after him:

"Come back here! Stop that boat! It's ours! Stop or we'll shoot!"

"Go ahead and shoot!" taunted Tom, hardly believing, after this delay, that they would go to this extreme. And they did not. Evidently their plan was to capture him alive.

Tom was so anxious to know whether or not his craft was keeping a sufficient distance in front of the other boat that he did not pay much attention to the course he was steering. The result was that, after he had swung out around a small island he was almost run down by a tug boat hauling some coal barges from one side of Lake Carlopa to the other.

Tom just had time to give the wheel a quick turn, and he fairly grazed one of the coal barges. This brought angry shouts from the captain of the tug who demanded to know:

"What in the name of thunderation are you trying to do, anyhow? Get yourself sunk? You soft-soaping landlubber, look where you're going!"

Tom did not reply. He had half a notion to swing about, run up alongside the tug and appeal for help. Then a wild desire came into his mind to beat these men alone and single-handed if he could. It would be sportier that way.

As for his pursuers, when they saw the tug and barges they appeared to hesitate a moment, as if ready to give up the chase. But when they saw Tom keep on, they did the same, still chasing him.

For perhaps ten minutes more the chase was kept up. Tom could make out, by hasty observations over his stern, that three of the men were in consultation while the fourth one steered.

There now loomed up in front of Tom another island—a larger one than Barn Door, and he recognized it as the last one in this end of the lake before he could swing into the wider part of the water through which there was a straight course to Shopton.

"Once I get past there," said Tom to himself, "I'm safe. They won't dare chase me after that."

As he neared the island he noticed that his motor was behaving in a peculiar manner. Every now and then it would miss an explosion. Then it would cough and wheeze a bit, after which it would go on again.

"What's the matter, old girl?" asked Tom, for to him machinery was almost something alive and he talked to it as he would to a human being. "Are you getting tired?" he asked.

He looked over the working parts. They seemed to be all right. But again came a miss—then several of them. And finally, with a last cough and wheeze, the motor stopped altogether.

"No more gas!" exclaimed Tom. Well he

knew that last wheeze when there is nothing more for the carburetor to feed on. He had used up the last drop of gasoline.

"Guess I'm done for," mused Tom. "They must have known there wasn't enough gas in the tank to carry me far. That's why they kept on." He looked back. The pursuers were perhaps five hundred feet astern, and Tom's boat was so close to the island that he knew, with the headway still on, he could reach the shore.

He turned the prow toward the little cove and as soon as he was near enough he leaped over the bow, landing on the rocky shore, and ran up into the fastness of the island, which was covered with scrubby trees and bushes.

He looked about for a good place where he might conceal himself. He was sensible enough to know that to try to fight four men was taking on odds that were too heavy. He saw a little recess in the rocks, and squeezed into it.

A moment later he heard the voices of the men as they steered their boat up against the one he had deserted. Then he heard them jumping out on the gravelly beach.

"We've got him now!" one remarked.

"He can't get away," added another.

"Not unless he swims for it—we've got both boats!" said a third.

"He won't try swimming—we could easily overtake him in our boat," declared the fourth scoundrel, and Tom sensed that this was true.

"Scatter now, and find him!" one of the men ordered, and the hiding youth could hear them crashing about in the bushes looking for him. It was a foregone conclusion that they would find him sooner or later. Tom had not had time to look for a good hiding place, being under the necessity of taking the first one that offered.

So it was no wonder that, a few minutes after he had landed on the island, he heard some one coming nearer and nearer. He tried to force himself farther into the crevice of the rocks, but it was no use. His movements dislodged some small stones which fell with a rattle.

"Here he is!" cried a voice.

The next moment Tom was looking into the leering face of Kenny, and then along came Schlump.

The latter held a revolver, and even without this weapon Tom would have been forced to submit, for the two masked men soon came to the aid of their companions. Tom felt that discretion was the better part of valor in this instance. Besides, he hoped, by submitting quietly now, to escape by strategy a little later.

But he thought he would try a little bluff and

bluster first, so he addressed the men with righteous indignation.

"You fellows have nerve!" he exclaimed. "What do you mean by treating me this way? I'll have you all arrested for this and sent up."

"Yes. Like you did Barsky, I suppose," sneered one of the masked men.

Tom started at the mention of that name. Barsky or Blodgett, for he used both names, had been concerned in the theft of Tom's Chest of Secrets. Barsky had been arrested, together with Renwick Fawn, and had been sent to jail.

"But maybe they have escaped," thought Tom. "Maybe these two men are Fawn and Barsky." He closely observed the actions of the men, but neither of them threw out his elbow in a jerky manner, which had been a characteristic of Fawn, nor were any of Barsky's peculiarities observable in the other masked individual.

"Cut out the talk," advised Kenny to the man who had mentioned Barsky's name.

"What do you want of me?" boldly demanded Tom.

"You'll find out soon enough," answered Schlump.

But his intention of keeping secret the reason for their bold acts was not shared by the masked man who had spoken of the imprisoned Barsky.

For approaching Tom and shaking his fist in the lad's face the scoundrel exclaimed:

"You're trying to beat us out of our invention, but it can't be done! We've got you now where we want you!"

"Your invention—what do you mean?" asked Tom, genuinely puzzled.

"The airline express car," was the unexpected answer. "That's our invention, and we're going to get patents on it ahead of you! We don't intend to let you cheat us out of it. You stole our ideas and models, but we'll use your models if we have to and get the patents that way."

"You must be crazy!" exploded Tom. "Your invention! You don't know what you're talking about! That car is my own and my father's idea! As soon as I get away from here I'll make you sweat for what you've done to me!"

One of the men laughed in a sinister manner.

"It will be a long while before you get away from here!" he boasted. "You'll stay a prisoner even if we have to ship you to the South Seas!"

CHAPTER VII

THE PLOT

CLOSING in on Tom, the four men soon had him securely bound with ropes. He felt there was little use in struggling against such overwhelming odds. He must conserve his strength until he could use it to better advantage. For the young inventor did not intend to remain any longer than he could help a prisoner of these four men on this lonely island. For it was a lonely island.

Though nearer that end of the lake where Shopton was located, still this little irregular circle of land, rocks, and shrubbery known as Loon Island was a lonesome place. Its name might indicate that, for in times past many loons made their nesting place on the island, and the loon is a very shy bird—it loves not human company.

"There isn't much chance of any one visiting here to rescue me," mused Tom to himself as he submitted tamely to being bound. That is, he submitted with seeming tameness, making no struggle. But, truth to tell, he was boiling within at the indignity put upon him and he was wild with righteous rage against the men for their threats to steal his idea of the great airline express.

However, there was nothing to do now but to let the four scoundrels work their will upon him. They were not unduly rough, but they took great care in the tying of the ropes. Then one of them noticed the ring of iron and the few dangling links on Tom's leg.

"He filed off the chain!" exclaimed one of the masked man. Like his companion he kept his face covered. As for Kenny and Schlump, they did not appear to mind being recognized. Perhaps they felt that Tom would know them even with masks on, so they did not go to the trouble to disguise themselves.

"I guess I have never seen the other two, and that's why they want to hide their faces from me," mused Tom. "They don't want me to recognize them again if I should happen to see them with their masks off. But I may, for all of that."

Tom had keen and observing eyes, and now, foiled in an attempt to see the faces of the two masked men, he began studying their peculiarities so he might know them again. He studied their walk, their actions, the way in which they used their hands and the tones of their voices. Often a person may be recognized by his voice alone. And Tom remembered how he had recognized Renwick Fawn by that man's elbow peculiarity. But he could not place these two.

"Yes, he filed the chain off all right," admitted Kenny. "We might have known he'd do something like that. We should have bound his hands."

"They're bound now," grimly remarked Schlump, as he tightened the knots on the rope around Tom's wrists. It was so closely drawn as to be painful, but Tom did not murmur. He was not going to let these men know that they were hurting him.

"We'd better take that leg bracelet off," went on one of the masked men, the larger of the two.

"Why so?" asked Schlump.

"Because the links on it might rattle just at the wrong minute," was the answer, and the man made a peculiar motion, pointing off to the mainland which Tom could see in the distance as he stood on Loon Island.

In a few moments the young inventor was freed from the leg-iron. It was not heavy, and gave him no particular discomfort, but, all the same, he was glad to be rid of it.

"Made me feel too much like an old slave on

the chain gang," he told himself. What the man had said about the necessity of keeping quiet on Loon Island came to Tom with force now. He had a wild idea of setting up a yelling that might attract some passing oarsman or motor-boat man. But he gave this idea up very soon.

"I might get help, and then, again, I might not," Tom thought. "If I didn't get it, these fellows would be angry at me and they might beat me up. I want to keep a whole skin as long as I can. I can do better work if I'm not injured. I wonder what their game is, any-how? It's a bold one—I'll say that. And to think I made it easier for them!"

For that is exactly what Tom had done. Thinking it over as best he could amid the whirl of ideas in his brain, he came to the conclusion that he had fallen into his present plight purely by accident. The men could not have known that he would follow that mysterious, disappear-ing stranger. They could not have known he would go down the flight of secret steps. But he had, through a chain of circumstances, and when the scoundrels found him in their power they proceeded with their plans. Tom had actually played into their hands.

Of course he might have escaped had the motor boat contained but another quart of gasoline, but this was one of the times when Fate played against the young inventor.

Having made their prisoner secure, leaving one of their number to watch him, three of the men went down to the two boats. Tom could hear them laughing as they discovered the plight of the craft he had jumped into.

"Good thing you were short on gas, Kenny!" some one said. "Otherwise he might be on the mainland now."

"Yes," was the answer. "Well, he'll be on mainland, anyhow, by night."

Tom wondered what this meant. But Schlump, who was guarding him, gave no sign.

All the remainder of that day Tom remained a prisoner on Loon Island with the four men watching him. They seemed to have some human feelings, for they gave Tom water to drink and loosed his hands so that he could eat some of the food they brought to him from the boat in which they had pursued him.

The prisoner was grateful for the food, and more so for the hot coffee, which Kenny made over a fire he kindled. This coffee put heart into Tom, and he felt much better after drinking it.

He was worried, not so much over his own plight, as over what his father and his friends might think about his sudden and mysterious disappearance. That his father would worry, Tom well knew.

But Tom would not give his enemies the satisfaction of asking them their intentions. He preferred to wait and see what would happen.

"They must be going to take me to the main-land," thought Tom, as he recalled what had been said. "It's hard to tell whether I'll have a better chance to escape there or here. I'll just have to bide my time."

It seemed that the day would never pass, but at length the shadows grew longer and Tom, who had been thrust into a rocky cranny behind a clump of bushes, realized that night was settling down. It would be the second night of his absence from home and he could imagine the anxiety among his friends.

"They won't know what to think," reasoned Tom.

Just before dark another meal was served to the prisoner, and then one of the masked men approached the young inventor with a gag in his hands.

"You'll have to wear this," he said roughly. "I wouldn't trust your promise not to yell when we're crossing the lake. I'm going to fix it so you can't shout for help!"

And this he did, binding Tom's mouth

securely. It was impossible for him to make himself heard five feet away. Then, when the ropes on his legs and ankles were looked to and made more secure, the prisoner was lifted by two of the men and carried to the larger boat— the one in which the scoundrels had pursued the youth.

He was laid down, with no great gentleness, on one of the side seats, and a little later, under cover of darkness, the trip from Loon Island to the main shore was begun.

Where he was landed Tom did not know—he could not see any familiar landmarks. Nor was he given much time to look about, for no sooner had he been carried out of the boat than he was bundled into a waiting auto and the machine was driven off over a rough road.

By the unevenness of the highway and by the damp smell all about him, Tom concluded that he was being taken through the woods. For an hour or more the journey lasted and then he saw that the machine had stopped in front of a lonely house set in the midst of the trees.

At the sound of the screeching brakes of the auto a door of this house opened, letting out a flood of light, and a voice asked:

"Have you got him?"

"We sure have!" answered Kenny. "Anybody been here?"

"Not a soul. It's as quiet as the grave. Take him right upstairs."

Before Tom quite realized what was happening he felt himself being carried up a flight of steps. He knew he was being taken into a small room, which, from the closeness of the air, seemed not to have been opened for a long time. He was placed on a pile of bags, or something soft on the floor, and a moment later his captors hurriedly left, locking the door behind them.

"Well, this is worse and more of it!" mused Tom, as he lay still a moment. He was on his back. His position was most uncomfortable and he began to roll over cautiously. He did not know but what there might be holes or trapdoors in the floor. He did not want to fall through.

He got over on his side and then, to his delight, he felt the gag loosening in his mouth. By rubbing it on his shoulder he managed to get free of it, and this was a great relief. He could breathe more freely now.

Moving cautiously around, his eyes saw a little sliver of light coming through a crack in the floor. Getting as near this as he could, Tom looked down. He saw below him, gathered about the table, five men. Two were Kenny and Schlump. The other two he saw were his other captors, the masked men. The fifth man seemed to be the keeper of the lonely cabin. They were talking in cautious tones, but the crack in the floor acted as a sort of speaking tube, and Tom thus heard mention of the plot against him.

"If we can't do anything else," muttered one of the men, "we'll blow up the Swift plant and those airline express models, too. Then there will be no question about us getting the patent. That's what we'll do—we'll blow up the plant!"

"When?" some one asked.

"To-morrow!" came the quick answer.

Tom felt a sinking at his heart. Here he was, bound and helpless, in the hands of his enemies who were hatching a vile plot against him and his father. Blow up the Swift plant! It was terrible to contemplate!

Tom began to struggle fiercely to release himself.

CHAPTER VIII

MR. DAMON'S NEWS

"BLESS my gasoline tank, I'm afraid I've done some damage!" cried Wakefield Damon.

"If you haven't damaged yourself you're lucky," grimly commented Ned.

"No, I guess I'm all right," said the eccentric man as he climbed out of his plane. He had managed to bring it to a level landing on the ground, though it was more by good luck than by good management.

He had flown over from Waterfield in the early morning, and either had not seen, or else had forgotten about, Tom's new mooring mast on the edge of the landing field. Straight for the big steel pole Mr. Damon had steered his craft, to swerve it at the last moment so that only one edge of a wing scraped it.

However, that impact was sufficiently force-ful to snap off the top of the mast and crumple the airship's wing.

"You got out of that pretty well," commented Ned, as he made sure, half by feeling and half by an inspection of the odd man, that he was not injured. A casual inspection proved, too, that the plane was not as badly damaged as at first feared.

"I'm sorry about that mooring mast," said Mr. Damon. "You must tell Tom to send me the bill for repairing it, Mr. Swift. By the way, where is Tom? I have some news for him."

He looked about the assembled group formed by Ned, Mr. Swift, Koku, and Eradicate. Something of their anxiety must have showed on their faces, for Mr. Damon asked:

"Has anything happened to Tom?"

"We don't know," answered Ned.

"We can't find him," went on Mr. Swift gravely. "Do you know where he is, Mr. Damon?"

"Me? No, I haven't seen him," was the answer. "But I have some news, just the same."

"News!" cried Ned. "What kind of news?"

"Not very good, I'm afraid. I'll tell you about it."

"How did you come to be flying so early in the morning?" Ned wanted to know.

"I came over specially to tell Tom the news," was the answer. "I thought flying would be the quickest way. I tried to telephone, but I couldn't raise you on the wire, Mr. Swift."

"We have been using the wires to communicate with different parts of the plant," said the old inventor. "That is probably why you could not get us. But I am anxious to hear anything about Tom."

"I wish I could give you direct news of him," went on Mr. Damon. "Bless my rubber boots! I'm so excited I hardly know which end I'm standing on—what with colliding with the mooring mast and all that! I wonder if I have damaged my new plane much?"

"Not much," Ned reassured him. "We can soon put it in shape for you. But you can hardly fly back in it, and you might as well come into the private office and tell what you know."

A little later, Koku and Eradicate having been sent to the house to tell Mrs. Baggert to telephone out to the works in case Tom arrived home, Mr. Swift, Ned, and Mr. Damon faced each other in the private office of the missing young inventor.

"What's all this about Tom not being found?" Mr. Damon wanted to know.

Quickly Ned told what had happened—that he had seen Tom outside the big fence, that the young inventor was expected to call on Mary, and that he had not appeared at the young lady's house.

"And since then we can't find a trace of him," concluded Ned.

"Well, what I heard a little while ago may serve as a clew," stated Mr. Damon. "Let me see now, where shall I begin?"

Ned was so impatient that he felt like telling the odd man to put on plenty of steam and begin anywhere that would give news of Tom.

But the "blessing man," as the old colored servant called Mr. Damon, must do a thing in his own way or not at all, and he was not to be hurried. So, having marshaled in his own mind what he wanted to say, he began:

"I have been away on a business trip and I only arrived home at two o'clock this morning. I got off the sleeper at the station, and, feeling hungry, I went into one of those lunch wagons across the street to get a bite to eat before going home and to bed.

"Well, while I was eating in this lunch wagon, and I must say the cook has a very clever way of frying eggs—while I was there two men came in—no, it was three men—wait a moment now, I can't quite be sure of that," and to Ned's exasperation Mr. Damon began examining his own recollection to make sure whether it was three or two men.

"Now I remember!" he exclaimed triumphantly, to Ned's great relief. "First two men came in, and then, later, a third. The first two were queer individuals—I thought they might be criminals, 'stick-up men,' you know, and I guess the fellow who ran the lunch wagon did, also, for I saw him slip his revolver out from a drawer and put it near the gas stove where he could get it in a hurry.

"But there was no need. The men were quiet enough. They ordered hamburger steak and onions—a vile combination, I'll say—and coffee. While they were eating the third man came in—now I have it right—and as soon as the two who had previously entered saw him one of them asked:

"'What about our quick friend?'

"'The speedy one is chained up where he can't do any harm,' is what the third man said. Then they laughed and the third man also ordered hamburger steak and onions and they began to eat as if they were half-starved.

"I didn't pay much attention to them at the time, for I was in a hurry to get home—I had told my wife I would arrive at midnight, but the train was late and I knew I'd have to explain why I was out at that hour. So I hurried up with my meal and was coming out when one of the men happened to say:

"'Well, this will put the airline express matter right in our hands!' It wasn't until then, as I was coming out and heard this remark, that I began to suspect something."

"The airline express!" exclaimed Mr. Swift. "Why, that's Tom's latest idea!"

"I know it is," said Mr. Damon. "That's what made me suspicious. Then I put two and two together—they had spoken about 'our quick friend,' and the 'speedy one,' and now I know by those words that they meant Tom."

"It begins to look like that!" cried Ned. "But what was it they said about him—that he was tied up?"

"'Chained up,' was the expression they used," Mr. Damon said. "I at once made up my mind that some of Tom's enemies were plotting against him and I decided to come right over and let him know. I waited a moment after coming out of the lunch wagon, and saw the three plotters disappear down a street that led to a wharf on Lake Carlopa. Then I caught a night-cruising taxi and made for my hangar. I decided to try to call you first by telephone, and, if I couldn't raise you to warn you to look out, I would aeroplane over and give the alarm.

"Well, I couldn't get you on the wire, so I roused my mechanic and we wheeled the plane out to my landing field. I didn't even bother to call up my wife, for I knew she wouldn't let me go, and I started off and—here I am."

"Lucky to be here, too, after hitting that mast," murmured Ned. "But what do you think this all means?"

"It means trouble for Tom, I'm sure of that," said Mr. Swift. "His enemies have captured him, I'm afraid. That's what that talk about being chained up means."

"It does look suspicious," agreed Ned. "We'd better start at the beginning again and make another search. We can do it better now that we have daylight. Tom has certainly disappeared in a very mysterious manner."

"You can count on me to help!" cried Mr. Damon. "Bless my police whistle, but I wish I had grabbed those three scoundrels when I had the chance! They have Tom a prisoner, I'm sure!"

"Hark!" suddenly exclaimed Ned, holding up a warning hand. "Some one is coming!"

CHAPTER IX

FOOTSTEPS could be heard coming along the hall that led to the private office where Ned, Mr. Damon, and Mr. Swift were conferring over the mysterious disappearance of Tom Swift.

"That isn't Eradicate or Koku," observed Ned, for well he knew the curious, shuffling gait of the colored man and the heavy tread of the giant.

"Sounds like a lady," announced Mr. Damon.

"Probably Mrs. Baggert," said Mr. Swift. "She will be terribly anxious about Tom—she's like a mother to him."

But it was not the kind, elderly housekeeper. A moment later Mary Nestor hurried into the room, her face and manner showing that she was worried and excited.

"Have you found Tom?" was her first inquiry, even before she nodded in greeting.

"No, Tom hasn't showed up yet," Ned answered with as much cheerfulness as he could put into his voice. "But he'll be along soon— we hope." He felt forced to add that last, for as the hours passed and no word came from Tom, even the optimistic Ned began to lose heart.

Then it was that Mary Nestor showed her true grit and spirit. Instead of sitting down and sighing or crying, she assumed a firm air and said:

"When he didn't come over last night I had a feeling that something had happened to him. I can't explain it, but I had that feeling. Now what have you done to find him, and what else remains to be done?"

"There's system for you!" exclaimed Ned admiringly. "Well, here's the situation." Then he related to Mary what they knew of the case, stating that he had met Tom the evening before just outside the big fence.

"Then that was the last any one has seen of him?" said the girl.

"Yes, the last, as far as we can find out," Ned answered. "When all the men report for work we will have each one questioned. It is possible some of them may have seen Tom after I did."

But this hope soon faded. A check-up of the entire factory force resulted in nothing.

"The next thing to do," decided Mary, "is to begin at the point where you saw him, Ned, and make a careful examination of the ground, to see if there is any evidence of a struggle. It is possible that Tom was overpowered and carried off soon after you left him."

"I don't see how that could happen without his giving an alarm," answered the young financial manager of the Swift plant. "But we'll go over that place with a fine tooth comb."

With the help of Mr. Damon and Mr. Nestor, who had followed his daughter, this was done. Of course Koku and Eradicate insisted on joining in the search, and had it not been that the matter was now getting serious it would have been laughable to watch the giant and the colored man. Each was jealous of the other, each was fearful that the other would be the first to discover Tom.

But nothing was found that would indicate in any way what had happened to the youthful inventor. The men who had used the secret flight of steps and the tunnel to carry Tom away had returned soon after overpowering him and had covered the opening to the underground stairs, scattering earth and débris over the planks so that a casual examination would disclose nothing wrong.

A closer inspection might have disclosed signs

of fresh earth scattered about, but this kind of examination was not made.

By this time every one connected with the Swift factory knew of the young inventor's disappearance, and work was ordered stopped for a time while a minute search was begun. Tom was looked for in all possible and in some impossible places, but all to no effect.

The day passed. Mary remained at the Swift house in order to be close at hand if Tom should return unexpectedly.

Ned began to look and feel blue and depressed when night came again and there was no sign of Tom. But, in contrast to this, Mary was outwardly more cheerful.

"Somehow," she said, "I feel that we shall have news of Tom before morning."

"What makes you think so?" asked Ned.

"I don't know—but I have that feeling," answered the girl. "You know if Tom has been caught and taken away, night would be the best time for him to escape, wouldn't it?"

"Yes, it would," admitted Ned. "But I can't believe that he has been captured."

"I can," Mary asserted. "I have had a feeling for some time that Tom would be in danger as soon as he tried to go ahead with that new invention of his—the airline express. It always

has happened so from the time he made his first
speedy motor boat until he put his valuable
papers in the Chest of Secrets. Always some
enemies have been on his trail. And you don't
imagine they're going to stop and let him alone,
do you, when he's got something as big as this
airline express almost perfected?"

"Well, of course there are always scoundrels
ready to take advantage of what an inventor
does," admitted Ned. "But this airline express
has been kept so secret I thought only a few
of us knew of it."

"That's what Tom hoped," Mary said.
"But only a few days ago he told me he had
had to discharge two men because he suspected
them. I forget their names—something like
Renny and Hemp."

"Kenny and Schlump," corrected Ned. "Yes,
he told me about those men. But still, and
with all you have said, I can't believe Tom has
been captured."

The day passed and night came. Mr. Swift
remained at the private office in the plant until
nearly ten o'clock, hoping that some word would
come from Tom; but none did, and an hour
later Mr. Damon insisted on taking the old
inventor home.

"Koku and I will stay here," volunteered Ned.
"And, after all, Tom is as likely to go home or

send some word there as he is to come to the plant. So we can divide our forces."

This was done, and Ned and the giant settled themselves down for the night's vigil. Several hours passed, and all was quiet at the plant. Ned was dozing when the big man, who had been sitting at a window from which' he had a view of the big fence, suddenly arose and whispered:

"Somebody come!"

"Somebody coming? What do you mean, Koku?" asked Ned.

"Man try climb fence," went on the giant, pointing out of the window. "Koku see him! Koku get him! Bust him all up in slats!"

"Wait a minute!" cautioned Ned, as he caught hold of the big man who was about to rush from the room. "No one can get over, through, or under that fence without setting off the alarm. It would ring here as well as in other parts of the plant, Koku, and the bell hasn't tinkled. You must have fallen asleep and dreamed it."

"Koku saw man on fence!" insisted the giant. "Maybe so him cut alarm wires."

"Even cutting the wires would ring a bell," insisted Ned.

"Maybe Master Tom hisself come and try get away from bad mans by climb fence," went on the giant, whose English left much to be desired. "Master Tom—he know how climb fence and no ring bell."

"That's possible," admitted Ned. "Tom rigged up the burglar alarm on the fence and he might know a way to beat his own game. Maybe you're right after all, Koku. We'll go and take a look. Where did you see the man on the fence?"

"There," said the giant, and he pointed out the place to Ned, who stood beside him in the open window. "Look—there him now!" cried the big man.

Ned had a glimpse of a figure trying to scale the high fence. In the darkness, illuminated only by a little light from the waning moon, the young financial man could not be sure whether it was a man or an animal. Even then he was wondering how it was possible for any creature to get up on the fence without sounding the alarm. And while Ned was thus wondering the alarm went off with a sudden clang that was startling.

"Now we catch 'um!" cried Koku, as he raced from the room, followed by Ned.

The alarm, ringing simultaneously in different parts of the plant, summoned a number of watchmen. As the alarm gave the location on the fence where the attempt had been made to scale it, the forces gathered there, Koku and Ned being the first to arrive.

But when a search was made with oil lanterns and electric torches no trace of an intruder could be found. The ground was hard and dry near the fence and no footprints were observed.

But Ned and the giant were sure an attempt had been made by some man to get into the Swift plant. That this was not Tom went without saying.

"They had Tom a captive somewhere," said Ned later, when he related the incident to Mr. Damon and Mr. Swift. "And thinking that with Tom out of the way it was safe to try to get in, that's what they did. But they didn't count on the electric alarm."

"I wish we could have caught that fellow!" murmured Mr. Swift.

"I'd 'a' kotched him ef I'd a bin dar!" declared Eradicate with a scornful glance at the giant. "Dat big man am too stiff to run! Better let ole 'Rad stay on guard de rest ob de night!"

"Hu!" taunted Koku. "Yo' so small burglar man eat yo' up!"

The remainder of the night brought nothing further—neither an alarm nor a capture. Morning came, the second day of Tom's disappearance, a disappearance that was just as strange as at first. Mary and the others were greatly worried now, and Mr. Swift was beginning to think that it would be best to notify the police and broadcast his son's disappearance.

It was in the afternoon, when Ned, Mr. Damon, Mary, and Mr. Swift were in the private office discussing plans, that the telephone bell rang. Ned made a jump for it, for though the signal had sounded several times during the day, each time only to have some routine work matter discussed over the instrument, still every time he heard the bell Ned felt certain it was a message from Tom. And this time his hopes were rewarded.

"Hello! Hello!" called Ned into the transmitter. Then, as he listened, what he heard made his eyes open wide with wonder. For over the wire came the voice of the young inventor himself, though faint and showing evidences of a great strain.

"Hello, Ned!" came from Tom. "I've just escaped! Watch the plant! Get Father to safety. Look out for bombs! I'll try——"

Then the voice died away to silence.

CHAPTER X

DESPERATION gave Tom Swift unusual strength as he lay bound and seemingly helpless in that upper story of the lonely cabin. Though the ropes about his wrists and ankles seemed very tight, he had a feeling as he strained his arms that he was going to get free. That talk he heard, floating up from the room below where, through the crack, he could see the conspirators gathered, gave him fierce energy.

"So that's their game, is it?" mused Tom, as he heard the plot to blow up the plant. "They want to put me out of the way so they will have a free hand to wreck my plant and get the plans and models of the airline express cars and airships. I don't believe they ever thought of inventing that sort of combination craft themselves. They are trying to steal my ideas. Kenny and Schlump must have hatched the plot. Oh, but I've got to get loose and warn Dad and Ned!"

78

It was this very necessity for quick action that emboldened Tom and gave him the fierce energy to struggle to get free of his bonds. He was glad the gag had come loose, for with that in his mouth, hindering his breathing, he could not have worked as hard as he did—he would have suffocated.

But now he could breathe easily, and he had need of all his spare wind in the exertions that followed the overhearing of the plot of the men who had captured him.

Luckily ropes, however strong, are capable of being stretched if one pulls on them long enough and often enough. And though it hurt Tom to force his bare wrists against the hemp strands, he kept at it until he found he could move his hands more freely. He wished he might find a projecting nail or some sharp object in his prison, against which he could rub his bonds to sever them. But he dared not roll about much for fear of making a noise and so bringing his captors upstairs. Once they discovered that he was making an attempt to escape, they might chain him fast or move him to some other prison whence it would not be so easy to get away.

"Once I'm free of these ropes I know I can get out," Tom told himself. "I'm only on the second floor, I can tell that, for I counted the stairs as they carried me up. And if I can get a window open I can jump to the ground, if I don't find some sort of a vine or a rain-water pipe that I can climb down. But the first thing to do is to get these ropes off my hands and feet."

Tom knew that once his hands were freed it would be a comparatively easy matter to loosen the ropes on his ankles. All his energies, then, must center on his hands. They were tied behind his back, with several coils of rope wound about the wrists. Again and again Tom strained on these until, at last, he felt that he could draw out one hand.

It was not easy, even when he had done this much, but he kept at it, and finally had one hand altogether freed. The exertion had made him sweat and had tired him greatly. He panted for breath as he lay there, while below him he could hear the murmuring voices of the plotters.

A little rest brought back Tom's breath and gave him renewed strength for what he had yet to do, which was to free his ankles. But he had accomplished the hardest part, which was to get his hands loose. It was not easy, however, to loosen the knots in the ropes about his feet, and it was several hours before he managed to free himself completely. One reason for this was the tightness of the knots, and another was that, occasionally one or more of the men below would come upstairs and flash a gleam from an electric torch into the room where Tom was a prisoner, to make sure he was still safe.

But the young man could tell, by the movement of chairs below, when this inspection was coming, and each time he was ready for it. He assumed on the floor the same position he had held when still bound and he wound the ropes back again on his wrists so it could not be seen, from a casual inspection, that they were loose.   And he also placed the gag in his mouth.

Because of the necessity for stopping work every now and then to assume the position of a bound prisoner, Tom was longer engaged in freeing his feet than otherwise would have been the case.

Consequently it was almost morning when he was able to stand up and move about freely. Cautiously he crossed the room, pausing at every board to make sure it would not squeak and betray him, and at last he reached a window through which the faint rosy streaks of dawn were coming—the second morning that Tom had been away from home.

"Now to see if I can get this window open," mused Tom.   He scarcely hoped to find that it would open readily, and he was not greatly disappointed when he found it fastened. By the morning light, now growing stronger, and by feeling, he ascertained that the sash was held down by nails driven over the edges of it into the frame.

A claw hammer would have taken these nails out in a second of time, but Tom had no claw hammer, and the files by which he had removed the chain from his leg had been taken from him.

"But maybe by bending the nail back and forth often enough I can either loosen it enough to pull it out or I can break it off," he told himself.

He felt that he must now work quickly. For some time there had been silence in the rooms below him, and he guessed that his captors were sleeping, thinking him securely bound and locked in.

"But they'll awake soon and start getting breakfast," Tom decided. "They'll bring me up some, and then they'll see that I have loosened the ropes. I've got to get away before they come up to feed me."

His fingers sought a wedging nail and began to bend it back and forth. At first it gave only a little, but eventually it moved more and Tom's hopes rose.

It was now getting lighter every minute.

Tom felt that each moment was precious. Unless he got the window open soon and could manage to escape through it, he would be discovered.

"There!" he exclaimed with a breath of relief as he at last broke off one nail. "Now for the other." The second proved easier, for after working it backward and forward a number of times and twisting it about, Tom pulled it out. Now the window could be raised, and this he did cautiously.

He waited a moment after lifting the sash and listened. There was no sound from below, and he thought that the men were still sleeping. He put his head out and looked down. To his dismay the window was higher above the ground than he had hoped, and there was on that side of the house neither a vine nor a rain-water pipe that he could descend.

"I've got to jump for it!" he grimly decided. "But that grass below looks soft." There was a big clump of green below the window. Tom climbed out, sat down on the sill, edged himself over and then hung by his hands a moment. This reduced the length of his drop by his own height. He hung there a moment and then let go.

Down he plunged, coming to a stop on the earth with a thud that shook him greatly. He seemed to lose his breath and a sharp pain shot through his left ankle.

"Guess I've sprained it," he mused. The pain was actually sickening, and made him feel faint. Through an open window on the first floor he heard some one exclaim:

"What was that noise?"

"What noise?" asked another.

"It sounded like some one falling."

"Guess you were dreaming! Get up and make some coffee. I'm half starved."

"All right," said the one who had first spoken. "But I'll just have a look at that bird upstairs. He's cute—maybe he's got away. I'll have a look at him before I get breakfast!"

"I've got to run for it—and right away!" thought Tom desperately. "Though how I'm going to do it with a sprained ankle is more than I know. But it will never do to let them catch me again."

The grass was tall and rank under the window. It would afford the fugitive cover until he could get to some better shelter. He began crawling through it, deeming this safer than trying to stand up and run. His concealment would be better in this position and it would take the strain off his hurt ankle. He hoped it was only a sprain and not a break.

He had not crawled more than a hundred feet

from the old house before he heard coming from it shouts that told that his escape had been discovered.

"Now I'm in for it!" he mused. Just ahead of him he saw a brook, not very deep but rather wide. "If I stand up and run they're sure to see me," he reasoned. "And if I crawl I'll leave a trail in the grass like a big snake. If I can get to the brook and crawl along in that I may throw them off the trail for a while."

It seemed the best thing to do, and while the men back at the house were running about "in circles," so to speak, Tom crawled to the brook, and then, having no particular choice, since he did not know where he was, he began crawling upstream. He did not hope to throw his enemies off his trail long in this way, nor did he. They were soon shouting as they ran down the grass-covered and weed-grown yard, for the open window had told them which way he had gone.

The trick of going into the brook confused them for a while, but Tom knew they would separate into two parties and soon trace him. He was desperate and at his wits' end when he saw just ahead of him on the edge of the stream an old barrel, partly embedded in the sandy shore. He could get into this without leaving the water, and as its open end was turned rather upstream he might escape observation.

It did not take him long to get into the barrel. He took care to leave no tell-tale trail, and his strategy was well carried out, for a little later, splashing their way upstream, ran two of the men—Tom could see them through a hole in the closed end of the barrel.

"But I'd better not stay here," the lad mused. "They're sure to come back, and the next time they might take a notion to investigate this barrel. I'll strike across country until I get to a house. There must be people living around here."

Tom never liked, afterward, to recall that journey. It was a painful one because of his injured ankle. He got a tree branch, which he used as a crutch and hobbled along on that. Once or twice he fainted and sank to earth in a stupor. How long these periods of unconsciousness lasted he could not tell. He dared not call out for fear of bringing the men on his trail.

Through the woods and across a swamp he pulled himself along, and at last, in the afternoon, as he could tell by the sun, he dragged himself out on a road and saw a white farmhouse a little way down it.

"I—I guess I'm all right now," faltered the exhausted youth.

It was a much surprised farmer who a little later saw a tall young man, obviously hurt, almost crawling up the front walk. Before the farmer could ask any questions Tom shot one at him.

"I've got to get an important message off at once. Have you a telephone? I'll pay for using it!" There was something businesslike in Tom's voice, weak and weary as it was, that impelled the farmer's respect in spite of Tom's rather disreputable appearance.

"Come in," the man invited. "Looks to me like you'd better telephone for a doctor while you're at it!"

"That can wait," gasped Tom. "Something else is more important. Show me the telephone!"

A little later he was gasping to Ned his message:

"Just escaped! Watch the plant! Get Father to safety. Look out for bombs. I'll try——"

Then Tom Swift fell over in a faint.

CHAPTER XI

THE EXPLOSION

DAVID KNOWLTON, the farmer upon whom Tom had called so unceremoniously, was scarcely more surprised by the sudden falling over of the young man in a faint than he had been at his eager request for a telephone.

"Great bullfrogs!" cried Mr. Knowlton, as he hurried to pick Tom up and lay him on a lounge in the room. "What's all this goings-on, anyhow?   What's it all mean?"

"Is he dead?" asked Mrs. Knowlton, who hurried into the room, having followed Tom and her husband when she saw the stranger come up to the house.

"I don't know, Sarah," was the answer. "But first hang that telephone back on the hook.   The inspector told me never to leave it off when we weren't using the line and I guess this fellow is through using it."

So the telephone went back on the hook, which defeated the plans of frantic Ned Newton, on the other end, if not to hold further talk with Tom, at least to learn from what station he was telephoning his message of warning. In vain did Ned appeal to the central operator to re-establish the connection.

"Unless you know the number of the party who called I can't connect you," she reported, and Ned knew, from previous attempts, that it was useless to carry the effort further. He could only hope that Tom would call again to relieve their minds. All they knew now was that he was alive, but that something dire portended.

Meanwhile Mr. and Mrs. Knowlton, kindly souls that they were, ministered to Tom Swift. The farmer's wife brought out her bottle of camphor, and a sniff of this potent spirit, with some rubbed on his forehead, soon brought Tom out of his faint. Then he was given a drink of water, which further helped in restoring his failing energies.

"If they come for me, don't let them get me!" begged Tom, sitting up on the couch. "Help me to get back! I must travel fast!"

"You need a doctor, that's what you need, young man!" decided Mr. Knowlton. "You aren't fit to travel. You've done too much of that already, from the looks of you, and that foot of yours is in bad shape," he added, as he saw the swollen ankle. Tom's shoe laces were almost bursting from the pressure of the swelled flesh, and the farmer had to cut them to loosen them. This gave Tom some relief, but the hardships he had gone through, the anxiety, and being without proper food so long, had so weakened him that he went off in another faint before he could tell his story.

"Call Doctor Prouty," advised Mrs. Knowlton. "We'll never get to the bottom of this until this young man is in his right mind."

Luckily the physician was in his office in the village and drove out in his car as soon as the farmer had telephoned. A hasty examination showed that Tom was suffering from exhaustion more than from anything else, and a little warm milk, followed later by more substantial food, soon gave the youth energy enough to tell the main points of his story.

"And if these men come after me—which they may do," he said to Mr. Knowlton, "you won't let them get me, will you?"

"I should say not!" cried Mrs. Knowlton before her husband could answer. "The idea! You poor boy!"

While the doctor was giving some directions as to what should be done for Tom, one of the hired men on the place came to the door of the room and reported:

"There's a couple of men outside who want to see you, Mr. Knowlton."

"All right—I'll see them," answered the farmer grimly. "Now don't you worry!" he told Tom, as the youth started to say something. "Just leave 'em to me."

Mr. Knowlton found two unprepossessing characters awaiting him on the side porch. He recognized them at once from Tom's description.

"Have you seen a young man passing here?" asked one of the twain. "He has escaped from an insane asylum and we want to take him back before he can do any damage. He has a delusion that he is a great inventor, named Tom Swift, and he will likely tell a very plausible story. Have you seen him?"

"Tom Swift is in my house now," said the farmer slowly.

"Is he? That's good! We're glad you have him safe!" cried the taller of the two men, with a quick glance at his companion. "Poor fellow—he needs care. We'll look after him. Much obliged for having taken him in."

"Wait a minute," went on the farmer, as the two men endeavored to push past him into the house. "Where are you going?"

"To get the patient and take him back to the asylum."

"Well, I'd wait a bit about that if I were you," went on Mr. Knowlton grimly. "Now look here," he went on, producing a shotgun from behind one of the porch pillars. "I'll give you fellows just one minute to run down the road and make yourselves scarce in any direction you like. Just one minute, and several seconds of that have already passed!" he added significantly, as he raised the gun.

"But I say—look here!" broke out one of the men.

"Half a minute gone!" said the inexorable farmer.

"You don't understand!" began the other plotter.

"I understand how to use a shotgun!" said Mr. Knowlton. "There's about fifteen seconds of that minute left and——" He cocked the gun.

But the two men did not stay to argue longer. With black looks and shaking their fists at the imperturbable farmer, they ran out of the gate, and with a grim chuckle Mr. Knowlton returned to Tom to tell what had happened.

"Thank you—a whole lot," said the young inventor. "They are desperate men. They are going to blow up my factory. I must get back at once and look after my father. He is an old man—he may not take my telephone warning seriously. Nor may Ned. I must go there myself!"

"But you aren't fit to travel!" expostulated Mrs. Knowlton. "One of the hired men could go."

"No, I must make the trip," decided Tom. "I'm all right now—except for my ankle. Have you an auto?"

"Oh, yes, we have a flivver," said the farmer.

"Then lend it to me—or sell it to me!" cried Tom. "I must make this trip at once—before night. Where is this place, anyhow?"

"You're in Birchville," was the answer. "It's about thirty miles to Shopton from here."

"I can make it!" cried Tom. "I can hobble along and make the trip in the auto. You'll let me go, won't you, Doctor?"

"Well, since you're so set on it, I reckon I'll have to. As you say, there's nothing much the matter except a sprained ankle, and if some one will drive the car for you——"

"I'll drive!" cried the farmer. "I want to see this thing through now. I didn't like the looks of those fellows with their lie about an escaped crazy man. I'll drive you home, Tom Swift!"

A little later they were on the road, and though the flivver made good time, still to Tom it seemed only to crawl. It was evening now, and rapidly getting dark.

Just before setting out he had again called Ned on the wire, telling his manager where he was, briefly relating what had happened, and again warning about the danger of bombs.

"Don't worry, Tom," Ned had 'phoned back. "We're so glad you're safe nothing else matters. But we'll be on our guard."

The lights of Shopton were in view. Mr. Knowlton drove his car down the slope that led to the Swift plant, the electric gleams of which could be made out now.

"I guess everything's all right," Tom said, with a note of relief in his voice.

But he had hardly spoken than there came the sound of a loud explosion.

"There goes something!" cried the farmer.

"I'm afraid so!" exclaimed Tom. "I wonder if that was at my plant? Oh, I do hope Ned and my father took all precautions!"

As the echoes of the explosion died away the little car carrying Tom and the farmer lurched forward.

CHAPTER XII

A DANGEROUS SEARCH

IMMEDIATELY after receiving the mysterious message from Tom, a message that seemed to come out of the air, Ned Newton made a frantic effort to get the operator at central to trace the call. But if one has ever tried to do this he knows how difficult it is. Unless one can give the telephone number of the party to whom he has been talking, and who made the call, if one is cut off there is little chance of the communication being re-established. Ned found this out to his sorrow.

"What is his number?" asked the telephone girl in a matter-of-fact way.

"His number? Great Scott, didn't I tell you——"

"I'll give you the manager," went on the bored operator.

But the manager could give no more satisfaction than his helper. He promised to trace the call and let Ned know what success he had.

"But I know what the answer is already," Ned remarked in disgusted tones as he gave up vainly rattling the hook. "We won't hear another word from Tom until he calls us himself. But we are sure of one thing—he's alive."

"Did he give you any particulars?" asked Mr. Swift.

"Bless my telephone book, who's been treating him this way?" demanded Mr. Damon.

Ned repeated the message as it came to him:

"Just escaped! Watch the plant! Get Father to safety! Look out for bombs! I'll try——"

Then the voice had died away.

"It's as we suspected," commented Ned. "He has been captured by some of his enemies and held a captive up to a little while ago. Then he got away. Good old Tom! You can depend on him for that!"

"But it seems to me we should do something," declared Mary, very much in earnest.

"Bless my eyeglasses, that's what I say!" cried Mr. Damon. "Come on—we'll get in my airship—it must be repaired by this time—and we'll rescue Tom! Don't lose any more time!"

"But we don't know where he is," said Ned. "It would be worse than useless to go scouring around the country looking for Tom in an airship. He might be only five miles from here or he might be five hundred."

"Yes," agreed Mary Nestor. "The thing for us to do is to follow Tom's advice—watch the plant, get Mr. Swift to a place of safety, and look out for bombs."

"Are you actually going to hunt through the plant for hidden bombs?" demanded Mr. Damon.

"Certainly," Ned answered. "It's the only thing to do after Tom's warning message. While I don't know what the game is, I think it likely that his enemies kidnapped Tom to get him out of the way so they could have a free run of the plant to search for and take away his models and papers of the newest invention— the airline express. Well, they got Tom, but he managed to escape, and their first attempt to sneak into the plant was a failure.

"Now they may have secreted some time bombs around the place. These may go off any minute, but, it is probable, they have been set to explode after dark. They hope to throw the place into confusion, and then to rush in and get what they want. But Tom has put us on guard."

"Yes," agreed Mr. Damon. "Then, as I understand it, we are now going to search for bombs that may go off at any minute?"

"That's right," assented Ned.

"Well, I'm glad I carry a large accident

insurance," said the eccentric man, forgetting to bless anything just then.

"Oh, there may not be much danger," Ned stated. "If the plotters hope to get Tom's models and papers it isn't likely they would use bombs of very great force. To do so would be to blow things so much apart that they couldn't get anything out of the ruins.

"So I think they will use bombs with only a small charge of explosive—enough to make a lot of noise, smoke, and confusion. But if we can find them first—the bombs, I mean—and put them out of business, we'll be all right."

"Yes," said Mr. Damon, "providing they don't find us first and put us out of business. It doesn't take much of a bomb to blow a man sky-high."

"No," grimly admitted Ned. "But that's the chance we have to take."

"Yes, it's a chance," said the odd man, and then he and Ned began their perilous work—for it was perilous in spite of what the young manager had said—while Mr. Swift and Mary Nestor returned to the house.

The heads of the various factory departments were called into consultation and instructions given them to search their respective quarters with minute care to discover any possible bombs. Koku and Eradicate were also called in and with Ned and Mr. Damon formed a separate searching party.

It was Koku who found the first bomb. The giant was looking in a pile of rubbish in one corner of a certain shop when he made a dive for something and cried:

"Cannon ball—like strong man throw in circus. I stronger than circus man—I toss cannon ball!"

Ned was just in time to stop him, for the giant had picked up a round iron object and was about to use it to exhibit his great strength when the manager cried:

"Hold it, Koku! That's a bomb!"

And so it proved to be—a bomb with a time arrangement for firing it, set to go off in about two hours. Ned quickly disconnected the firing arrangement and the bomb was put in a pail of water.

Efforts were redoubled to find the dangerous "cannon balls," as Koku called them, and in a short time three more were discovered in various parts of the plant. They were all set with time fuses which had more than an hour yet to run, so the bombs were rendered harmless with no ill effects to the searchers.

But it was when the shadows of evening were falling, and Ned and the others had about given up expectation of finding more bombs, that Ned unexpectedly came across one hidden in a refuse box outside of Tom's private office.

It needed but an instant's look to show that this was timed to go off almost immediately, which fact, when Ned discovered it, caused him to shout:

"Look out! This is a live one!"

He hurled it from him, toward a pile of lumber in the shop yard. There was a deafening report—a shower of planks and boards rose in the air and settled back again with a crash, while a cloud of smoke filled the air.

"Just in time!" cried Ned. "If that had gone off here it would have killed all of us."

And as the echoes of the explosion died away a voice was heard shouting:

"Is any one hurt? Father, are you there? Ned, is any one hurt?"

CHAPTER XIII

AN OMINOUS MESSAGE

Curious, indeed, was the chance, coincidence, or fate—call it what you like—which brought Tom Swift on the scene, in company with Mr. Knowlton in the runabout, just as the bomb which Ned tossed away exploded near the lumber pile. Tom and his friend felt the force of the blast, but, aside from a stunned feeling and the shock, they were unhurt, and after a momentary stopping of the car Mr. Knowlton sent it on again.

But Tom was anxious to know what had happened; hence his cry as he saw the flash and heard the blast so near his plant and his volley of questions as soon as Mr. Knowlton brought the car to a final stop. And Ned, hearing his friend's cry, first marveled and then rejoiced.

"Tom! Tom!" he shouted. "Are you there?"

"Yes," was the answer. "But what happened? Is my father all right?" There was so much smoke from the bomb that Tom could not see far ahead, especially as it was now dark.

"Your father is all right—he's back home with Mary," Ned informed Tom, as the latter got out of the car to limp toward the entrance gate near his private office. "And the plant isn't damaged. Come in and I'll tell you about it."

"Are these your friends? Are you sure everything is all right?" asked the cautious farmer, as he saw Tom preparing to go in through the big gate in the high fence. One of the men had hastened to open it when it was certain that Tom was outside.

"Yes, everything is all right," was the answer. "This is my factory—my friends are here. But my enemies have been trying some of their tricks. Luckily the tricks didn't work. But don't go," begged Tom. "I want you to meet Ned Newton and my father. He'll want to thank you for aiding me—for bringing me back here."

"Oh, shucks! That wasn't anything!" expostulated Mr. Knowlton. "Anybody would have done the same. I won't stop now. I'm in a hurry to get back home—my wife will be worried. But she'll be glad to know you got here safe and found your friends. Come out and see us some time."

"I will," promised Tom, and then as his benefactor drove away, Tom and Ned rushed toward each other to shake hands, while Mr. Damon brought up the rear, murmuring:

"Bless my insurance policy! Bless my rubber boots! If this isn't most astonishing!"

"Are you all right, Tom?" demanded Ned, anxiously looking over his chum. "But you're hurt!" he cried.

"Only a sprained ankle," explained Tom, who was hobbling about. "I had to jump out of a window. But is Dad all right? What was that explosion?"

"One of the bombs you warned us about. We found four—this was the fifth and just about to go off. I fired it away not a second too soon. It chewed up some of your spare lumber. I guess it's the last. But where have you been? After the first message of yours we didn't know what to think until you telephoned again that you were on your way in. What's it all about?"

"Trouble, I guess," answered Tom. "Some gang is after me and the new airline ideas and patents. They're desperate. Wait until I 'phone to the house to let Dad and Mary know I'm all right, and then I'll explain. Why, hello, Mr. Damon!" Tom exclaimed as he saw his eccentric friend. "Did they get you over here to hunt bombs?"

"He overheard some talk which gave us an idea of the desperate men who were after you," stated Ned. "He came over in a hurry, and——"

"Too much of a hurry, I guess," broke in Mr. Damon, in rather crestfallen tones. "I smashed up your mooring mast, Tom."

"That's a small matter—easily mended. I'm glad you weren't hurt. I'll tell you everything in a few minutes."

Tom limped into his office and soon was conversing with his father and then, at more length, with Mary. They were rejoiced to learn that he had escaped and was safe. Then began the telling of the two-sided story—the events leading up to the explosion of the bomb Ned had hurled away just as Tom arrived.

Tom related how he had seen the strange man disappear behind the bush, how he had followed, had gone down the secret steps, and how he awoke out of a doped stupor to find himself a prisoner. Then he told of being taken to the lonely house and how he had escaped.

Ned, in turn, related their anxiety when Tom did not come home, and told how they had searched for him before and after the arrival of Mr. Damon.

"We sure were glad to hear your voice over

the wire," Ned stated. "But somebody cut us off."

"No, I fainted," Tom explained, "and Mr. Knowlton or his wife hung up the receiver without trying to carry on the talk, which, if they had done, would have told you everything. But the doctor soon pulled me around and the only thing really the matter with me now is this swollen ankle. But that will soon go down and then I'll get after these fellows and finish work on my airline express. Now tell me where you found the bombs."

Ned did, stating that one had been found near Tom's office.

"Well, there may be more bombs," Tom said. "I won't be satisfied until we have gone over all this plant again. We can't afford to take chances. But I'll move my airline express models and patent papers—that is, the preliminary ones—to a place of safety in my Chest of Secrets."

This was done, and then another careful search was made of the premises. No more bombs were found and Tom announced his intention of going home to get some much-needed rest.

"But how do you suppose, with all your guards, Tom, and the electrical fence, those fellows planted the bombs?" asked Mr. Damon.

"I don't know," replied the young inventor. "I'm afraid there is treachery somewhere in our working force. Without the aid of confederates those plotters couldn't have put the bombs in here. I'll have to make an investigation. But for the present the danger is past, I think."

They were all in need of rest and quiet after the exciting two days through which they had passed, especially Tom, and when he reached home Mrs. Baggert insisted on putting him straight to bed, in which place, to tell the truth, the young inventor was not at all averse to spending some time.

The following day things had rather quieted down at the plant. The resulting débris was swept up, and the shattered lumber pile, devastated by the bomb, was examined for remnants of the infernal machine. Several pieces of cast iron were picked up, and Tom said he would investigate them to try to discover, if possible, where the bomb was made. It appeared to have contained no missiles, being merely a hollow shell filled with explosives, set to go off at a certain time, and Ned had hurled it away not an instant too soon.

"The first thing we've got to do," decided Tom, a few days later, when he was able to be about without his crutch and with much of his former energy restored, "is to investigate that

secret stairway. Maybe some of the fellows are
still on Barn Door Island."

But the delay, short as it was, had given the
plotters time to vanish and to destroy some
of their work. The stairs were in place, but
after tearing up the planks, after the soil had
been swept away, there was revealed only a
blind passage. The tunnel had been caved in
a short distance from the secret steps and it
was impossible to traverse it.

The same conditions prevailed on Barn Door
Island. The place where Tom had emerged
from the tunnel was found, but a short distance
back in the passage dirt and rocks were piled
up, preventing a further examination being
made.

"Maybe they're walled up in the tunnel under
the lake," suggested Mr. Damon.

"Not likely," Tom said.

"They probably cleared out after their bold
plan didn't succeed," Ned remarked.

"Yes, they've gone for a time," Tom admitted. "But that doesn't mean it's forever.
They're still at large and they won't give up so
easily. I'm afraid for the success of my airline
express plans. But I'm going to work on
them."

That Tom's fears were well grounded was
borne out a few days later when, as the young

inventor sat at his desk, his private telephone rang. Tom's own instrument had a number not in the book and was known only to a few. Unless this number were given to the central operator Tom's 'phone bell would not ring.

But ring it did on this occasion, and over the wire came this ominous message:

"Look out for yourself, Tom Swift! We'll get you yet!"

CHAPTER XIV

THE AIRLINE EXPRESS

LIKE a flash Tom Swift realized that this warning had come from those daring enemies of his who were still at large—the same men, Kenny and Schlump and the two masked ones, who had kidnapped him. He could realize their rage at his escape, their anger at the foiling of their plot to blow the place up by bombs, or, if their intention was not to cause serious damage, but only confusion, during which they might rob—this, too, had been frustrated.

For a moment the sinister character of all that had taken place stunned the young inventor. The danger under which he was, came to him with a sickening realization and he sat for a moment holding the receiver in his nerveless hand.

He was brought back to a sense of realities by hearing the somewhat distant voice of the operator asking:

"What number, please?"

That stirred Tom into action.

"Look here!" he cried into the instrument. "You don't realize how important this is! I've received a threat over the wire! I must trace——"

"Hold the line," interrupted the girl in a matter-of-fact tone, and, for a moment, Tom felt hopeful that he could thus get on the trail of those who sought to injure him. But while he was even thus hoping another voice broke in on his thoughts saying:

"This is the manager, have you any complaint to make?"

"Oh—no!" exclaimed Tom in despair, realizing how useless it was to try to trace the call thus. He was going through much the same experience Ned had gone through the time Tom called him from the farmhouse and then fainted. "I'll call and explain. This is Tom Swift speaking," he told the manager. "I want to trace a call that came over my private wire, but I can do it best by a personal visit, I believe."

"We will do all we can for you," the manager said, for she knew the Swift concern was a large and important one. "It is often difficult to trace stray calls that may be made from any of a hundred pay stations. But I will help you all I can."

"Thank you," said Tom, and hung up the receiver. Then he fell into deep thought.

As he had feared, the danger was not over. His enemies were only biding their time. They had failed in their first efforts, but they were not going to give up. The sinister threat was enough to disclose that.

Deciding that quick action was the best way to trace the mysterious call, Tom at once summoned Ned and they visited the local telephone exchange. There the records were gone over, but aside from establishing the fact that the call was put through from the Waterfield central, nothing was established. From just what station the threatening man had spoken, Tom could not find out. That it was a man's voice he was certain, but whether or not it was one of the four or five who had held him prisoner in the lonely house Tom could not decide.

"But there's something in the fact that the call came from Mr. Damon's town," said Ned. "And he overheard men talking about you the time he was eating in the lunch wagon. It begins to look, Tom, as if the headquarters of the gang was in or near Waterfield."

"Yes, it does," agreed Tom. "I think we'll take a run over there. I want to see Mr. Damon on business, anyhow. And we can take in that old house where they had me tied up. I want to see if I can get any clews there."

However, a visit to the lonely shack, which

Tom located after some difficulty, was without result. It had long been uninhabited, and the owner, when found, said he knew nothing of the men who had been in it. This Tom and Ned could well believe. A search through the premises revealed nothing of any value as a clew. The ropes which Tom had discarded when he made his escape had been taken away, or it might have been possible to trace the place where they had been bought.

"I guess Waterfield is our next and best hope," remarked Ned, as he and Tom came away from the lonely house.

"I think so," agreed the young inventor. "Mr. Damon may have heard something more."

They found the odd man contemplating his new plane, which had been repaired and taken back to his own private hangar.

Mr. Damon led his visitors to his private office, and there Tom told the latest happenings. But Mr. Damon was unable to throw any light on this new development, nor was he able to trace the men he had overheard talking in the lunch wagon. He had tried to get the police to locate them, but without avail.

"Well, we'll let that go for the present," decided Tom. "Now for something else—my latest idea, so to speak. I heard you say, the other day, Mr. Damon, that you had some loose funds you wished you could invest in a paying undertaking."

"That's right, Tom, so I have, bless my bank-book!"

"Well, I'm thinking of forming a company to exploit my airline express. I find that a large part of Father's funds and mine are tied up in such a way, in our other inventions, that I can't get enough ready cash in a hurry, and I need considerable to start this new method of travel. I thought perhaps you might be interested."

"I think I may be, Tom," said Mr. Damon. "Tell me about it."

"Well, it's like this," began the young inventor. "You know over in Europe and here, too, though to a much more limited extent, great interest is being manifested in travel by aeroplane—I mean travel by private parties. They have aeroplanes now that carry ten or twelve at a time over the English Channel. You can also fly from Paris to Berlin and between other European cities. In fact, they have regular routes of travel there. But here we have only a few which might be called experimental if we exclude the air mail which is a great success between New York and Chicago and western points. Now what I plan is this: An airline express from New York to San

Francisco, a straight-across-the-continent flight by daylight—say from sunrise to sunset."

"What do you mean, Tom?" cried Wakefield Damon. "Do you mean to tell me you can build an aeroplane that will cross the continent in twelve hours?"

"Not in twelve hours, perhaps," replied Tom, with a smile. "Though I'm not ready to admit that's impossible. But there are more than twelve hours from sunrise to sunset—or rather, from dawn until dark. I'll set the time at sixteen hours. That ought to be easy."

"But you spoke of making the trip continuously—without change," said Mr. Damon, to whom Tom's idea was not altogether new. "None of the aeroplanes we have at present can do that—it's all of three thousand miles. The British transatlantic fliers didn't make as long a journey as that, though of course they were in more danger, flying over the ocean."

"Probably it wouldn't be a non-stop flight," said Tom. "The air mail doesn't do that— different planes are used. It's just the same in making a transcontinental trip in a railroad train. No one engine makes the entire trip, nor does a single train crew. But it is possible to get in a sleeping car in New York and stay in the same car until you get to San Francisco. The car is merely coupled to different engines, made up into different trains at certain designated places."

"Is that your plan?" asked the odd man. "I thought you said you were going to run aeroplanes, not railroad cars."

"I am, if I can make a go of it," replied the young inventor. "But it will be a combination aeroplane and railroad coach. Here is my idea in a rough form."

He laid before Ned and Mr. Damon a sketch of a large and powerful plane and also a sort of coach on wheels. The two were shown separately and in combination.

"You see," went on Tom, pointing out the different features, "the passengers would take their places in this coach—a sort of glorified automobile—at the first landing field, on Long Island. There this car, which will hold half a dozen or more, will be fastened to the aeroplane by clamps. The aeroplane will take off, and make an airline for Chicago, which will be the first of two stops to be made between New York and the Pacific coast. Landing on the Chicago field, the autocar will be detached and rolled, under its own power, to the second aeroplane which will be in waiting. It will be clamped fast to the chassis, and if the passengers happen to be asleep they will not be awakened, any more than they would when a Pullman sleeper is taken off one train and put on another.

"As soon as the car is clamped to the second plane that one starts and flies to Denver. There it descends, the car is rolled to the third plane, in waiting, and that sets off, landing in San Francisco about sixteen hours from the time the start was made—a daylight trip across the continent."

"Can it be done?" asked Mr. Damon.

"I think so," Tom answered. "I plan now on making one trip each way every week. There will be three laps of approximately one thousand miles each. Figure five hours to a lap, that would mean a flying rate of two hundred miles an hour—not at all impossible. We'll charge a fare of one thousand dollars each way. There'll be money in it, Mr. Damon. Do you want to go in with us?"

Instead of answering Mr. Damon rose and tiptoed his way softly to the door, where he stood intently listening.

CHAPTER XV

A TRIAL FLIGHT

TOM SWIFT and Ned Newton watched the odd man curiously. Afterward Ned said he thought Mr. Damon had gone to the door to ascertain if his wife might be eavesdropping, since she did not altogether approve of many of the things he did in connection with the young inventor.

"I thought maybe he was going to get his checkbook," Tom said later. He was always a very hopeful individual.

But when Mr. Damon returned to his seat after his tiptoeing visit to the closed door he remarked in a low voice:

"You can't be too careful."

"About what?" asked Tom, impressed by his friend's manner.

"About letting your plans become known before you are ready to spring this new airline express on the public," was the answer.

"Why, you don't suspect any one in your own house, do you?" asked Ned.

"Not my wife, of course," Mr. Damon answered. "But there have been several queer characters around here of late. Several men have called, trying to get me to hire them as a valet. Bless my necktie, as if I needed a valet! Of course I sent them away, but yesterday the maid let another one in while I was busy in my study, and the fellow had the impudence to walk right up to my door. My wife caught him standing there listening after the maid had gone away, and Mrs. Damon sent the fellow flying, I'll tell you.

"I suspect, Tom, that he had something to do with the gang that is trying to get your new apparatus away from you. He must know that I am your friend and often go on trips with you, and possibly he thought he might get some information here, in a sneaking way. That's why I wanted to make sure no one was out in the hall listening. It's all right. I looked out through the crack and no one is there. Now go on with your explanation."

Tom did, elaborating on his plans for a big aeroplane in two sections, the part where the passengers were to be carried being like a big autocar, able to move under its own power.

"It is this feature that will save a lot of time," he explained. "After the first aeroplane starts from Long Island the passengers will not have to move out of their seats until they reach San Francisco. Or, if we start at night, in case it is found desirable to have overnight trips, a man can go to sleep in New York and awaken at the Golden Gate, that is, if he wants to sleep that long."

"It's a big undertaking!" said the odd man.

"But Tom can carry it through if any one can," declared Ned.

"The worst of it is that it's going to take a mint of money," sighed the young inventor. "That's why I'm calling on you and some of my other friends to take stock, Mr. Damon. How does it strike you?"

To the credit of Mr. Damon be it said that he did not hesitate a moment. He held out his hand to his friend and said:

"I'm with you, Tom Swift! I'll invest all I can afford. I wish it was more, but I've spent a lot on that new aeroplane of mine that I nearly smashed. However, I have a few dollars left in the bank. Though you needn't say anything to my wife about this," he went on in a low voice as he got out his checkbook.

Tom and Ned smiled as they gave a promise of secrecy, and a little later the young inventor left with his first contribution toward financing the airline express—a check for five thousand dollars.

Tom Swift spent busy days during the next few weeks. Like all new enterprises, this one was not easy to start, though many of Tom's friends, whom he approached with a plea that they buy stock which would pay big dividends if the plan succeeded, at once purchased blocks. Others required more persuasion, and not a few said they would buy stock if they could see the machines in operation.

"That's what we've got to do, Ned," decided the young inventor, when it was evident that the enterprise might fail through lack of capital. "We've got to show these Missouri birds that we can fly this combined auto and aeroplane. Gee, I'm sorry now Dad and I have all our ready money tied up in those other matters."

"But can you build a trial machine?" asked the treasurer of the Swift concern.

"I can as soon as my patent papers come through from Washington," Tom said. "That's where the hitch is now. After all the machines we have made in our plant, it would be queer if we couldn't build a speedy aeroplane of extra power and also a chassis to clamp on to carry the passengers. That's where the patent comes in—the method of combining the two."

"But I understood that the patents had been allowed," said Mr. Damon, who was present,

"That was the latest advice from your Washington lawyer."

"Yes, I know. But several matters have come up since then. Some one is trying to throw a monkey wrench into the gear wheels, so to speak, and I suspect it is the same gang that tried to put me out of the way—the scoundrels headed by Schlump and Kenny. I think I shall have to make a trip to Washington myself."

"Be careful, Tom," warned Ned Newton. "They may get you on the way there."

"I guess I can look out for myself," was the answer.

But when Mary Nestor heard what Tom proposed to do, she added her warning to Ned's. However, Tom was firm and then Mary delivered her ultimatum.

"If you go to Washington, I'm going, too," she declared.

"Good!" cried Tom. "I've been wanting a little excursion with you, Mary, and we'll make a party of it and take Ned and Helen along. That will be fun!"

"That's the idea!" Ned declared. "It will be a bold gang that dares to start anything with the two girls along."

It may be mentioned here that Tom's patents were really of a three-fold nature. One consisted of the peculiar construction of the passenger car to be used in the ocean-to-ocean flight, the second was a patent on the method of clamping this car to the aeroplane, and the third covered the method of manufacturing the duralumin alloy of which the car and a part of the aeroplane were to be constructed. Ordinary duralumin is composed of ninety-four per cent. aluminum and the rest copper and magnesium; but Tom had a secret formula of his own, not only for mixing these ingredients, but also in the melting and forging processes. His duralumin he considered stronger than any ever used in an aeroplane and it was at least three per cent. lighter in weight than any which had ever been offered to him.

There is nothing like going yourself when you want a thing done, as Tom found, and he had not been many days in Washington, whither his three friends accompanied him, before he had matters connected with his patents straightened out and he was assured by a high government authority that his claim was original, valid, and would eventually be allowed, thus giving him the sole right to make airline express machines for a limited period.

Perhaps this action of the patent authorities was hastened when an old army officer, a friend of Tom's father, heard about the matter and declared such a machine would be of great value to the United States in case of another war.

This officer impressed his views on certain friends of his in the patent office, and the result was that the usual leaden wheels in that institution began to move more rapidly.

"If you can wait long enough," said General Malcolm, who had been of such service to Tom, "I believe I can even get you a government subsidy."

"How long would it take to get the government to invest money in this new undertaking of mine?" Tom wanted to know.

"Oh, probably two or three years. A bill would have to be introduced in Congress—it might take four years."

"I expect to make the first flight inside of a month," Tom laughed.

Tom and his friends returned to Shopton, and then followed many strenuous days and nights of work for the young inventor. Those who had faith in Tom and those who knew and understood Ned Newton's unusual knowledge and judgment in financial matters so talked to their friends that eventually outsiders put one hundred thousand dollars into the scheme and this, together with the money Mr. Damon and other acquaintances subscribed and with what Tom and his father had, gave them enough cash to build three planes and two cars.

Essentially there was nothing new or startling in the construction of either of these machines. My readers are all familiar with the general outline of an aeroplane. Beneath the fuselage which held the engine and a cockpit for the pilot and his helper was built a heavy frame to which could be clamped the passenger car.

This car was like a Pullman parlor car combined with a sleeper. It had some folding berths and also some easy chairs. There was a small dining room and a buffet kitchen, and many conveniences were installed. Tom limited the number of passengers to be carried on any one trip to ten, saying he could enlarge the cars if he found the machine was going to be a success.

In due time the two cars and the three planes received their last coats of varnish, the powerful engines were installed after a rigid block test, and one day Tom announced to Ned that all was in readiness for a trial flight.

"Want to come along?" asked the young inventor.

"Sure!" was the quick answer. "Anybody else going?"

"Yes. Mr. Damon is game and Father insists on accompanying us. I think I'll take Koku

along—he might come in handy in case anything should happen."

It was decided to make the start from the
big field outside of the Swift plant, and one
morning one of the planes and its accompanying
passenger car was rolled out on the level
stretch. To make the test under the same
conditions that would prevail when the airline
express was in service, Tom and his friends
entered the passenger car at one end of the
field.

"We will imagine," explained Tom, "that
we have just landed here from the plane that
brought us from Long Island to Chicago on the
first lap of the transcontinental flight. Now
we will run over and attach ourselves to the
other plane."

As has been said, the passenger car could
move under its own power, as can an automobile.
Tom started the motor and skillfully guided the
car under the waiting aeroplane. In a moment
workmen had fastened the clamps.

"Let her go!" Tom called to the pilot in
the aeroplane, and the big propellers began to
revolve with a thundering sound. The engine
seemed working perfectly and a moment later
the whole machine—the airline express—began
to roll forward across the field. There was a moment of doubt as to whether or not the aeroplane

would raise itself and the heavy weight it had to carry, but Tom had made his calculations well, and, to his delight and that of his friends, the machine began to soar upward.

"Hurray!" cried Ned. "She's doing it!"

"Yes, we're off on the first real flight, anyhow," agreed Tom.

"It works better than I expected," Mr. Swift said. All along he had been a bit skeptical about this new scheme.

A little later they were sailing over Lake Carlopa and Mr. Damon, looking down from one of the observations of the car, said:

"Aren't we flying a bit low, Tom?"

"Yes, I think we are," agreed the young inventor. "Put her up a bit!" he signaled to the pilot through the speaking tube.

Back came the answer:

"I can't! Something has gone wrong! I'm losing power! I'm afraid we're in for a fall!"

CHAPTER XVI

JASON JACKS

JUST for a moment or two Tom Swift wished he were in the motor cockpit of the plane instead of in the passenger car with his father and his friends. He had an idea he might so manipulate the controls as to cause the falling plane to increase speed and keep on flying until a safe landing could be made.

But in an instant this idea passed. Tom had full confidence in his mechanician, and realized if Harry Meldrum could not prevent a fall Tom himself could not, for Meldrum, taught in the Swift school of flying, was a thoroughly competent and resourceful airman.

"What's wrong?" Tom asked his engineer through the tube.

"Oil pump has blown out a gasket! The engine is heating. It's got to stop soon and we'll have to come down—in the lake, I guess," was the grim finish of the report.

"Well, I've landed in worse places," remarked Tom.

"Is anything going to happen?" his father wanted to know.

"I'm afraid there is," the young inventor answered. "We're being forced down. I thought everything was all right with the machinery, but you never can tell."

"Bless my accident insurance policy! do you think we'll go down right in the water, Tom?" gasped Mr. Damon.

"It begins to look so," was the reply. "But perhaps better there than on land—there won't be such a shock. The plane has floating compartments, and so has this car—I had them built in as a precaution against water landings. I don't believe there will be any real danger."

There was no doubt about it—the plane was gradually settling lower and lower—ever coming nearer to the surface of Lake Carlopa.

"She's slowing up, Tom," remarked Ned, as he listened to the throbs and pulsations of the motor above them.

"Yes, I'm afraid we're in for it," came the response. "Can't you make any emergency repairs, Meldrum?" he asked the mechanician.

"Bert's trying, but it doesn't seem of much use," was the answer. Bert Dodge was the assistant engineer, and fully as competent as his chief.

"This settles one thing," remarked Tom, as he glanced out of the car window. "On the next flight I'll have a duplicate oiling system installed."

"Brace yourselves, everybody! We're in for a ducking!" came the cry.

The next moment the big new aeroplane and its attached passenger car plunged into Lake Carlopa with a mighty splash. For a moment it seemed that they would be engulfed and all drowned before they could make egress from the plane and car. But Meldrum had guided the machine down on a long angle so that the water was struck a glancing blow. In effect, the lower surface of the car and the tail of the plane slid along the surface of the water for some distance. This neutralized some of the force of the impact, and then, though the machine settled rather deeply in the water, it did not sink. The air compartments prevented that.

However, help was at hand. A number of motor boats were out on the lake, their occupants watching the trial flight of the new airline express. When it was known that an accident had happened, these craft speeded to the rescue. As soon as the boats drew near the men in the plane and those in the car climbed outside and thence were taken off in the boats.

"Looks as if it was going to be a total loss, Tom," said Mr. Damon gloomily, as the craft settled lower and lower in the water.

"It's bad enough," Tom admitted, ruefully shaking his head, as the boat that had taken him off circled about the *Falcon*, as Tom had christened his first machine. "But even if she sinks to the bottom I believe I can raise her. The lake isn't very deep here."

However, it was not quite as bad as that. The *Falcon* was only partly submerged, and there she lay, water-bound, in the lake. Her actions decided Tom to install more air-tight compartments and make the car lighter, which would insure its floating higher in case of another water drop.

"Well, there's nothing more we can do now," decided the young inventor. "If you'll take me ashore, please," he said to his rescuer, "I'll make arrangements for getting the *Falcon* out."

He gave orders to this effect as soon as he reached his shop, and when Mr. Swift, with a dubious shake of his head said:

"I'm afraid this is a failure, Tom! It's too much for you," the young inventor with a determined air answered:

"I've never given up anything yet, and I'm not going to begin now! I see where I made some mistakes and I'm going to correct them."

And when the plane and the car were raised and brought to shore—being found to have suffered little damage—Tom started his reconstruction work with more vim than before.

However, the accident, while it was not a serious one from a mechanical standpoint, had a bad effect on Ned's campaign to raise funds for putting the airline express into actual service. True as it is that nothing succeeds like success, nothing is more dampening to a money campaign than failure. Capital seems very timid in the face of failure, and deaf ears were turned to Ned's urgent appeal to the public to buy stock. For while Tom was working on the mechanical end, Ned looked after the business interests.

"Well, Ned, how goes it?" asked the young inventor at the close of a hard day's work when Tom himself had been much cheered by the progress he had made in lightening his passenger car and installing a dual oiling system on the plane.

"It doesn't go at all," was the somewhat gloomy answer. "People seem afraid to risk their money. If you could only make a successful flight, Tom, or get some millionaire to invest about a hundred thousand dollars without really seeing the thing fly, we'd be all right."

"I think I'll be more successful in the first

proposition than in the second," replied Tom, with a smile. "I don't know many millionaires who are letting go of dollars in hundred thousand lots."

"In fact, Tom, we're almost at the end of our financial rope. We've got just about enough to complete the improvements you have begun."

"After that I'll try another flight. If that succeeds I think public confidence will be restored," returned Tom. "If we fall again—well——"

"You'll give up, I suppose," finished Ned.

"Not at all!" was the quick reply. "You'll find some other means of financing the thing. This is going to succeed, Ned! I'm going to make it! We'll go from ocean to ocean by daylight!"

Tom banged his fist down on his desk with force enough to spill some ink out of the bottle, and then, getting up from his chair, began putting on his coat.

"Where are you going—out to hunt for a kind millionaire?" asked Ned.

"No; that's your end of the job. I'm going for a ride with Mary," was the smiling reply. "I want to get some of the cobwebs out of my brain. I can't do any more now, and I promised Mary I'd take her for a spin in the electric run-

about. It's working all right, I suppose?"
he asked, for Ned had been using that speedy
machine in his financial campaign.

"Yes, it works well, Tom—faster than ever.
And I hope things will take a turn for the
better to-morrow."

"So do I. See you later," and Tom was off
to keep his appointment with Mary Nestor.

Tom and Mary were riding along a quiet
country road back of a little village when Mary
observed just ahead of them an old man driving
a horse hitched to a light carriage.

"Speaking of millionaires, Tom," she said,
"there goes one."

"Where?" he asked.

"There! Jason Jacks. He has several
millions, it's said, but he holds on to them.
Father knows him."

"Lucky boy!" exclaimed Tom. "I wish I
were you, J. J.!"

"Well, I don't!" came promptly from Mary.
"If you were Jason Jacks, I wouldn't be out
riding with you, Tom Swift!"

"Why not?" he demanded quizzically.

"Because he's old, he hasn't any teeth——"

"Well, you don't want to be bitten, do you?"
joked Tom.

"No, of course not. But he's got a mean
disposition, he's homely——"

"Thanks!" interrupted Tom, with a laugh. "That's an implied compliment, I take it."

"Take whatever you like," laughed Mary.

"I'd like to take a few thousands from Millionaire Jason Jacks," retorted the young man. "Still, if you feel that way about him, Mary, I'm just as glad to be what I am," and Tom—well, it is affairs of no outsider what he did just then.

The look which passed between him and Mary changed in a moment to a glance of alarm as the girl pointed to the carriage ahead of them and exclaimed:

"Oh, Tom! I believe that horse is running away!"

"I pretty near know it is!" was the answer, as Tom began to speed up the electric runabout.

"Oh, Mr. Jacks will be thrown out," went on Mary. "He doesn't seem to know how to manage that animal! And there's a dangerous part of the road just ahead—it goes around a curve and close to the edge of a cliff! Oh, Tom, what are you going to do?"

CHAPTER XVII

THE AIRLINE STARTS

MARY NESTOR'S reason for putting her question to the young inventor was because Tom was speeding up the electric auto and guiding it along the road in the direction of the runaway horse. For that the animal was in a frenzy and was now running away was apparent to both the young people.

"What are you going to do, Tom?" repeated Mary.

"I'm going to save Mr. Jacks if I can before he gets to the dangerous part of the road," answered the young inventor. "If I can run up alongside of him, I may be able to lift him out of his carriage in case there is a likelihood of his going down the gully. Is the road very narrow there, Mary?"

"Yes, it is—hardly wide enough for two between the side of the cliff on the left and the edge of the gully on the right."

"Then there's not much chance of driving

the runabout between him and the edge of the
gully," reasoned Tom. "I might go in myself.
Luckily he's driving on the left side of his buggy
and this car has a right-hand drive. I can reach
right over and grab him. And when I get near
enough to do that, Mary, I want you to take the
steering wheel of this car and hold it steady.
Can you do that?"

"I'll try, Tom."

"You've got to do it if we're to save his life."

"Very well then, Tom, I will," returned Mary
in a quiet voice, and Tom knew she would not
fail him. "How fast the horse is going!" she
added.

The light buggy whirled around a curve on
two wheels in a manner to make Mary catch her
breath. Tom gave a low whistle. Then as
the runabout made the same curve, Tom saw
that the road ahead was straight but narrow.
On one side, the left, rose a high cliff of rock,
and on the right hand was a deep gully, the
road running along its very edge.

"Oh, Tom, do you think you can catch him
in time?" asked Mary anxiously. "There's
another curve, just ahead, and if the horse goes
around that as fast as it is going now it will go
over the edge and Mr. Jacks will be killed!"

"I've got to get him before that happens,"
declared Tom grimly. "The horse will never

be born that can beat my runabout." Not idly had Tom's electric machine been called "the speediest car on the road," and now it surely was speeding.

Though the frantic horse did his best, it was naught against the power of the batteries concealed in Tom's car, and in a few moments the young inventor was driving along the narrow road on even terms with the swaying carriage in which sat a white-faced man. He was sawing on the reins and trying by his voice to halt the horse, but without effect.

"The curve is just ahead, Tom," warned Mary.

"All right," he answered. "You take the wheel now. I'm going to stand up, reach over, and pull him into this car. Keep close to the face of the cliff—it's our only chance!"

A moment later Tom rose in his seat, and as his hands left the steering wheel Mary leaned over and took charge of guiding the car. Exerting all his strength, Tom caught hold of Mr. Jacks under the arms and fairly pulled him from his seat. Luckily the old man was frail and light, or Tom could not have done it.

"Here! Here!" cried the frightened horseman. "What—what——"

But the breath was fairly choked out of him as Tom hauled him into the runabout and jammed

him down on the seat between Mary and himself. Then Tom grabbed the wheel, and put on
the brakes with all his might, for the dangerous
curve was just ahead.

On sped the maddened horse, the buggy
bouncing up off the uneven road. Just as the
runabout slowed to a stop the mad animal swung
around the curve. It did not make it, for its
speed was too great, and a moment later Mary
gave a cry of pity as the ill-fated brute shot over
the edge of the cliff, dragging the light buggy
with it. There was a rattle of gravel, a shower
of stones, a weird cry from the horse, which
must have sensed its doom, and then the end
came.

Down the precipitous cliff had plunged the
animal, crashing to death on the rocks below
amid the splinters of the little carriage. Up
above on the road, close to the rocky face of the
cliff, sat the three in the runabout—a trembling,
aged man, a white-faced girl, and Tom Swift,
flushed by his exertions.

"Well—well," stuttered Jason Jacks, when he
could get his breath, "I guess I've had a narrow
escape. My—my horse went over the cliff,
didn't he?"

"I'm afraid he did," answered Tom grimly.

"Well, I'm just as glad," went on the millionaire.

"Oh, Mr. Jacks!" exclaimed Mary.

"Ha! you know me, do you, young lady? Well, the reason I said that is because if he's that kind of an animal, likely to run away without warning on a dangerous road—as he did—I don't want ever to drive him again, and I wouldn't want anybody else to. I only bought him the other day, and I'm glad I found out his trick in time. But let me see—you know me. Do I know you?" and he glanced sharply at the now blushing girl.

"I think you know my father, Mr. Jacks," she replied. "He is Mr. Nestor, and I have seen you at our house."

"Oh, of course! To be sure—Mary Nestor. Well, I'm much obliged to you—and more obliged to this young man for saving my life. What's your name?" he asked bluntly.

"Tom Swift."

"Tom Swift. Oh, yes, I've heard that name before. You have a plant in Shopton, haven't you? You make motor boats and such things?"

"Yes, I have invented a few things," Tom modestly admitted.

"Um—yes," murmured the millionaire. "I've heard of you. Well, I'm too much upset to thank you properly now. Could you leave me at my home?"

"Glad to," answered Tom. "Do you want

to drive around the road at the bottom of the cliff and find out about your horse?"

"I guess there isn't much left of him, young man," was the grim answer. "He's had his last run. It was a narrow escape for me. How did you happen to be right on the spot?"

"Just by chance," Tom replied.

He drove back to the millionaire's home, declining an invitation to come in. Then Tom and Mary went on, and when later in the evening he left her at her home, she said with shining eyes:

"Oh, Tom, suppose he should?"

"Should what, Mary?"

"Give you ten or twenty thousand dollars for saving his life? He could well afford to do it— he'd never miss the money—and then you could finish the new airline machines."

"I don't want any reward for saving lives, Mary. Besides, he'd have to give you a share. If you hadn't been with me I never could have saved him."

"Nonsense, Tom!"

"No nonsense about it!"

It was the next day that Jason Jacks called at Tom Swift's office, driving up in a handsome two-horse carriage with a footman in livery. For the old millionaire was eccentric and liked to imagine he was living in the old times. He never could be induced to ride in an automobile.

"I've come to reward you, Tom Swift, for saving my life," began Mr. Jacks, taking out his check book.

"Excuse me, sir," said Tom, firmly but in respectful tones, "you can't do anything of the kind."

"Can't do what?" Mr. Jacks asked sharply.

"Reward me for saving your life. Any one else would have done the same if he had had the chance, and I would have done the same for any one else."

"Yes—I suppose so," slowly admitted Mr. Jacks, and it was easy to see that Tom's refusal pleased him rather than otherwise. "Human life can't be bought, though I hold mine at a high price. But look here, young man, since you won't accept a reward, will you let me do you a favor in return for the one you did me? That's fair, isn't it?"

"Yes, I suppose it is," admitted Tom.

"Well, then, I've been making inquiries about you, and I hear you are trying to launch a new invention. I don't go in much for those things myself—I have no use for aeroplanes, motor boats, or automobiles, though I admit they have their place in the world, and I own stock in several motor companies. But I won't ride in them.

"Now, I hear you are contemplating an airline express to San Francisco, but you haven't had much success with it so far. Am I right?"

"Yes," admitted Tom. "I have no hesitation in saying I am a bit short of cash to complete some improvements."

"Then will you let me help finance the thing?" asked Mr. Jacks. "Oh, on a strictly business basis," he added quickly, as he saw Tom about to refuse. "I'll buy stock the same as I would in any other enterprise, and if it succeeds I expect to be paid my profit, the same as other investors. If it fails—well, it won't be the first time I have lost money, though I don't make a practice of that," and he chuckled dryly.

"I'd be glad to sell you some stock," said Tom quickly.

"All right then, young man, we can do business. I'll have my secretary see you in a few days. I don't like to be under obligations to anybody."

"Neither do I," retorted Tom; "and I feel sure that you will get a good return on what you invest with me. I'm going to succeed."

"Well, if you do half as cleverly as you did when you pulled me out of that runaway, you'll win!" predicted Mr. Jacks.

A few days later he invested fifteen thousand dollars in Tom's new enterprise, taking stock to that value, and promising that if Tom could make six successful trips each way, between Long Island and the Golden Gate, carrying passengers as arranged, he would invest one hundred thousand dollars more and perhaps even a larger sum.

"Hurray!" cried Tom when he heard this news from Ned, who, of course, had attended to the details of this matter. "Now our success is assured!"

"Oh, I'm so glad!" exclaimed Mary, when he told her.

Busy scenes were the order of the day and night at the Swift plant after this much-needed new capital was paid in. Tom kept his men busy making improvements in the *Falcon*, and at last the day arrived when a final test was to be made.

Once more Tom, Ned, Mr. Damon, Koku, and some others took their places in the car. Mr. Swift declined to come, saying it was too much for his nerves. The car rolled over the field, was clamped to the chassis of the big aeroplane, and up in the air it rose.

This time there was no accident, and off above the lake and over the country soared the *Falcon*, flying beautifully. "It's a success!" cried Ned.

"I want to make a test landing and see how long it takes to unclamp the car and fasten it to the other plane," said Tom, before he would permit himself to exult.

This test was successfully met, and up rose the second plane, carrying the car, just as if the scene had taken place on the field in Chicago, the end of the first lap of the proposed airline express.

Not until then did Tom permit himself to see visions of complete success. But after another landing had been made and when the car had been rolled to the third plane, it was evident that the scheme could be carried out. The third plane did not go up, not being quite ready.

"Of course," Tom said to his friends when they were talking it over, "this doesn't mean that we can make the time which I hope is possible—sixteen hours from coast to coast— but I'm going to make a big effort for those figures."

In the next few weeks matters were rushed to completion. A landing field was secured on Long Island, another in Chicago, one on the outskirts of Denver, and the last one at the Golden Gate. The route was mapped out with care, and guide posts and signal towers were placed in position.

Then, on a certain day, after many exhaustive tests, it was decided to inaugurate the first schedule of the airline express. The two planes had been sent, one to Chicago and the other to Denver, while the third was waiting on the Long Island field, where the passenger car had been taken.

Newspaper reporters, camera men, moving picture operators, and many spectators were on hand.

"All aboard!" cried Tom, as he gave the signal to start. As he was about to close the door of the car, which would soon be soaring aloft, a boy ran across the field and thrust into the hands of the young inventor a piece of paper.

"What is it?" demanded Tom.

"Message for you! Man gave me a dollar to deliver it just as you started," panted the boy.

Then, before he could answer, though he had an ominous feeling, Tom felt the car being lifted off the ground. The airline express had started!

CHAPTER XVIII

CHICAGO

STRANGE and mingled were the feelings Tom Swift had as his great experiment was started. There was exultation mingled with apprehension. Exultation that he had at last triumphed over many difficulties and the plots of his enemies and had reached the point of starting the service which might revolutionize travel. Apprehension lest he might fail, and also apprehension over this latest happening—the giving to him of this note.

It had a sinister appearance—this hasty message delivered in such a manner. It was in keeping with some other things that had happened of late.

But Tom's chief concern now was to see that his new craft got safely into the air and on its way. He could deal later with those who sought to steal from him the fruits of his labor and his brain.

So, overcoming his natural curiosity to see

what the note contained, Tom resolutely thrust it into his pocket and gave his whole attention to directing the management of the *Falcon*, which was the plane and accompanying car selected to hop off on the first leg of the transcontinental trip. The other planes were named, respectively, the *Eagle* and the *Osprey*.

This last name was chosen by Tom as fitting for the plane in which he hoped to ride when he sighted the Pacific coast and ocean. For the osprey is a fish-hawk, and Ned agreed with Tom that it was a most appropriate name for a craft in which they hoped to sight an ocean with its millions of fish.

Tom, together with Ned, Mr. Damon, and some assistants, rode in the hanging car, while in the cockpit of the aeroplane above them were Harry Meldrum and Bert Dodge, the two able mechanicians. Once he had seen for himself how the car behaved, Tom intended to take his shift in the cockpit, piloting the plane part of the time.

Tom had invited Mr. Jacks to make the first trip, but the eccentric millionaire, whose money had enabled the initial planes to be finished and who had promised to invest a hundred thousand dollars more in case Tom could successfully complete six round trips, had smiled as he shook his head.

"None of that for me!" he had answered. "Runaway horses are dangerous enough, without tempting fate in the shape of an aeroplane. I wouldn't go up for a million dollars, Tom. But I wish you all success!"

And success is what Tom hoped for as the craft rose from the ground on this, its first official trip.

"Well, Tom, she's moving!" exclaimed Ned, as they rose higher and higher on a long slant off the landing field and headed toward the west.

"Yes, we got off in good shape," agreed Tom, as he noted various instruments and gages on the walls of the car which indicated their speed upward as well as forward and gave their height above the earth.

"It certainly is fine," asserted Mr. Damon. "Bless my upper berth! it beats traveling in a Pullman. And if you can do as you say, Tom, and keep us in this car right through to the end of the journey in San Francisco, it will be a marvel. No change, nothing to worry about, and traveling as clean as in a bath tub! It's great! Bless my toothbrush, it's great!"

"I wouldn't go so far as to say there was nothing to worry about," remarked Tom, with a laugh, as he signaled to the mechanician for more speed.

"What do you mean—that letter the kid gave you?" asked Ned, in a low voice.

"No, I haven't looked at that yet. Probably it's from some one who begged for a free ride," Tom answered. "But I mean the race isn't over until we have sighted the Golden Gate. We've got to be there before dark to make a success of this airline express, and we've got to travel pretty fast—averaging two hundred miles an hour for over fifteen hours. I hope we can do it, but I haven't given up worrying lest we fail."

"Oh, we'll do it all right!" declared Mr. Damon.

"Sure!" added Ned, though, truth to tell, he could understand and appreciate Tom's feelings, knowing, as he did, something of mechanics and the slight defect in a piece of machinery that might throw all calculations out.

The *Falcon* was now rapidly gaining height and speed, though, comfortably housed as they were in the car, the occupants felt no unpleasant sensations.

If one has ever ridden in an aeroplane he knows the swift, easy, gliding motion of the car. It is like nothing on earth, for there is absolutely no motion felt as in riding in an automobile or motor boat. There are none of the bumps of the roads, nor the swaying or rolling of water travel.

Of course there are "air pockets," and when these are encountered even the best airship may take a sudden drop, which sensation is slightly felt. And if one exposes one's face or hands or other part of the body to the rush of air, there is a most distinct sensation felt. But the cowl of the cockpit protects those in it from the terrific rush of wind, the pressure of which, at two hundred and six miles an hour, is tremendous; and of course those housed in the car felt nothing.

So it was like making a journey in a dream, almost, and once the passengers were up above the earth there was nothing by which their progress could be gaged, as there is in a railroad train, when telegraph poles, fence posts, and the scenery seem to rush past at great speed.

So perfectly were the powerful motors running that in a short time the gages showed that the great speed of two hundred miles an hour had been attained. But Tom wanted to do better than this, especially on the first part of the journey, between Long Island and Chicago.

"The more time we make on the start the less we'll have to worry about when we begin on the third lap—over the mountains," he said to Ned. "I'll go up into the cockpit myself soon. I just want to see that everything is all right here."

This did not take long. A full complement of passengers was not carried on this initial trip, and there was more than room for all of them in the comfortable chairs. Koku had to be content with a bench, for no ordinary chair was large enough for him, and to his delight Eradicate was allowed to take charge of the small kitchen, where a buffet lunch would be served at noon, and other refreshments as needed.

"Ah eben gib dat giant suffin in case he git hungry," chuckled Eradicate, who seemed to forget his jealous enmity against the big man in his delight at being near Tom and allowed to serve.

After making a round of the car and seeing that everything was well, Tom signaled up to Meldrum that he was going to take charge of the driving of the plane, asking Meldrum to come down below. There was an enclosed companionway, or ladder, by which the plane cockpit could be reached through the roof of the detachable car.

"Hadn't you better look at that note before you go up?" suggested Ned, motioning to the pocket in which Tom had put the letter the boy had delivered to him at the last minute.

"That's so—I almost forgot about it," said the young inventor, with a laugh. "But it's too late to answer it—we're quite a way from the starting point."

This was true. It had taken only a few minutes for them to soar over New York City, with its forest of tall buildings, then over the Hudson, across Jersey City, and so out on the long straight air line that led to Chicago.

Tom pulled out the crumpled missive and ripped open the envelope. As he read the few lines a look of anger came over his face.

"What is it?" asked Ned.

"Read it yourself," Tom answered.

And Ned scanned these lines:

"Look out for yourself. You have started but you haven't finished. Our time is coming.
"The Masked Two."

"Well, of all the nerve!" cried Ned.

"Haven't they!" said Tom. "But it will take more than threats to make me give up this project. I haven't got my final patent papers, but I will when I finish these trial trips. I need to make only five more after this, and then Jacks will put in a lot of money. It was lack of ready money that was holding me back— once I have plenty of cash I can snap my fingers at those fellows!"

"Only five more trips," murmured Ned. "And this one hasn't finished its first third, Tom. But we'll do it! The Masked Two can go jump in the lake."

"You said it!" exclaimed Tom. "I'm not going to worry any more about it. Come on up in the plane with me."

But though Tom declared that he was not going to worry over the matter, still he could not altogether dismiss it from his mind. He had left his aged father at home in charge of the works, and though there were faithful men around him and every safeguard that ingenuity could devise, still those sinister enemies might find some way of breaking through the cordon and damaging the plant or injuring Mr. Swift. So, in spite of his brave words, Tom worried.

"However, we're in touch with them all the while by wireless," Ned remarked, as Meldrum and Dodge descended when Tom had assumed charge of the controls, with Ned to help him. "You can always send and receive messages, and so you'll know when anything happens."

"Yes," agreed the young inventor. "I almost forgot about that. I can keep in touch with home that way. I'll wireless back soon, and see how everything is."

This Tom did after he had speeded up the plane a little, once he found the motor was working well after warming up. They were now high in the air, hastening west.

Ned sent off the message through the ether waves. A powerful radio set had been installed, and Tom could talk directly to his father, which he was soon doing.

"We're making fast time, Dad," he told him. "How are things back there?"

"All right, Tom. You made a fine start. I only hope you keep it up."

"We will. And look out for yourself. Our enemies haven't given up."

"I'll be on the watch, Tom. Good-bye and good luck!"

For over four hours Tom and Ned, by turns, with occasional relief from Meldrum and Dodge, kept the motors running at top speed. And it was not quite mid morning by the clock when Ned, taking an observation, cried to his friend:

"There's Chicago below us, Tom!"

"Good!" exulted Tom Swift. "We'll finish the first leg a little ahead of time!"

CHAPTER XIX

DENVER

Tom, by his calculations and by computing their rate of speed for the past five hours, was already pretty sure in his own mind that they would reach the City of the Lakes at least within the time limit he had set for himself. But he was, nevertheless, glad of Ned's confirmation.

"Now if they have everything in readiness at the field, we won't lose much time in detaching this car from the *Falcon* and in hitching it on to the *Eagle*," Tom remarked to his chum as he prepared to make the landing.

"It wouldn't do any harm to wireless them and make sure," Ned suggested.

"No, you're right. Go ahead and do it. And, by crickity grasshoppers!" cried Tom, as he looked at the gasoline and oil gages, "we're getting in just by the skin of our teeth, too."

"How come?" asked Ned.

"We've got just about enough gas left to make the field," Tom said. "I didn't realize we'd used up quite so much. The engine was cold when we started so early in the morning, I guess, and it took more fuel to pep it up. I'll take along a bit extra on the next two legs."

"A good idea," suggested Ned, as he began working the wireless instrument, to call the operator at the Chicago landing field. He was not long in getting him, for Tom had made his arrangements well, and those associated with him in the airline express were anxiously awaiting his arrival.

"We'll land in about three minutes," Ned sent the message. "Is everything in readiness for a quick change?"

"All O. K., sir," was the reply, for a former army flier was in charge here and he held to the traditions of the service.

"Better send word back to Dad," went on Tom, as he banked the plane slightly in readiness for bringing it up into the wind to make the landing on the big field just below them. Off to the left was the glistening lake, and Tom had a momentary glimpse of the wide and beautiful Lake Shore Drive, Chicago's principal boulevard.

"Did you get him, Ned?" asked the young inventor, as he noted below him the crowd that had assembled to await his landing. Word of the sensational attempt to link the two edges of the United States by a dawn-to-dark flight had been broadcasted all over the country.

"Yes, your father's all right," reported Ned, who had been listening. "He sends his congratulations and so does Mary."

"Is she there?"

"Yes, and anxious for your success," reported Ned.

"Tell her I'll talk to her after we hop off on the other leg," directed Tom, and then his attention had to be given to making a safe landing—no easy feat when it is remembered that he had no ordinary aeroplane to bring down, but a heavy car attached to it and passengers to look after.

But he was successful, letting the *Falcon* gently down to the ground with scarcely a perceptible jolt, and then rolling gently along the even field toward the place where the other plane was in readiness, with motors slowly turning over.

"Lively now!" cried Tom to the men who gathered about him—trained workers from his own shops who had been sent on ahead to make the changes. "Every second counts, boys!"

A curious crowd surged forward to see the daring men who had set out to do their best to annihilate time and space. The throng would have overwhelmed the plane and its occupants, thus preventing the quick shift of the car, but for the fact that mounted police, whose aid Tom had enlisted, kept the curious ones back a certain distance. As it was, however, there was another small army of movie cameramen, newspaper photographers, and reporters on the scene, anxious to get the news.

"Will you please stick your head out of the window, Mr. Swift! Thanks. There! I got you!" Thus spoke one of the newspaper cameramen. Meanwhile others were clicking their shutters while the movie men were industriously grinding the cranks of their machines.

"What were your sensations? Did anything happen on the trip? Do you think you'll make the next leg on schedule?"

These were only samples of the scores of questions that were fired at Tom by the newspaper reporters as he sat in the car while it was being unclamped from the first plane ready to run, under its own power, to the other plane a short distance away.

Tom answered as best he could, while Meldrum piloted the car carefully through the mass of men eager for information. They were the only ones allowed to approach closely, for Tom well knew the value of newspaper and movie news-real publicity. He wanted his venture to be well known, since he needed much capital to put it on a paying basis, and the more people who knew about it the better chance he would stand of getting capital into the venture.

So Tom, and Ned occasionally, answered all the questions, gave a brief summary of the first thousand miles of travel and told something of their expectations.

"All ready?" called Tom anxiously, as he looked at his watch. The change was taking a little more time than he had counted on.

"All ready, sir!" came the answer.

"Let go!" Tom called to his new mechanician Sam Stone, who, with his helper, Jim Waldo, was to do most of the driving on the second lap of the journey. Of course Tom would take the wheel now and then to relieve the pilot, who was, necessarily, under a great strain.

The throttles were opened and the twin motors responded with a thundering volume of explosions which sent the *Eagle* across the field at ever increasing speed, carrying the car and its passengers with it. Then, like some great bird, true to her name, the *Eagle* rose into the air.

Chicago seemed to drop rapidly below the passengers as the plane mounted higher and higher, and her nose was pointed due west. Tom took anxious observations of the various gages, noted the increasing speed, and seemed well satisfied until he scanned the weather reports which one of his assistants handed him. They had just come in from the government observatory in Denver, and as Tom laid them back on the operator's table there was a worried look on his face.

"What's the matter?" asked Ned.

"There's a report of storms ahead," was the answer. "But we may be able to go above them. Strong head winds, the report says. They are likely to delay us. But we won't worry until we have to. And now what do you say to something to eat, Ned?"

"I'm in favor of it," was the answer. "We had breakfast a bit early," which was true enough.

"Then tell Rad to serve up what he has," directed the young inventor to another colored man who had been brought along to wait on the table, since Eradicate insisted on doing the cooking.

It was nothing new for Ned, Mr. Damon, and Tom to eat while traveling at high speed far above the earth. They had made many trips in dirigible balloons and other craft, sometimes remaining up almost a week at a time. But this was the first occasion where so much depended on long-continued speed, and the meal which was soon served was more or less interrupted as Tom left the table to ascertain what progress they were making.

On the whole, it was satisfactory. As hour

after hour passed, the time being whiled away by communicating back to Shopton now and again —Tom holding his promised conversation with Mary—it began to look as if the great project would succeed. It was an hour after lunch when Tom, peering down toward earth through a pair of powerful binoculars, announced with exultation:

"There's Denver!"

"On time, too!" exclaimed Ned. "Tom, we're going to make it!"

They had just come down from the plane cockpit, where Tom, with Ned's help, had been guiding the craft.

"Yes, it looks as if we had two-thirds of our journey behind us," the young inventor was saying when from the galley came the cry of Eradicate:

"Fire! Fire! She's on fire!"

CHAPTER XX

A MOUNTAIN STORM

Tom Swift had to think of many matters when he planned his airline express. He was aided, however, by his past experience in manufacturing aircraft and he had made many journeys above the earth and had been in many kinds of peril.

Not the least of these were fires, and Tom well realized the danger of ignition in a craft necessarily so frail as a flying machine heavier than air. So in building the *Falcon*, the *Eagle*, and the *Osprey* he had taken into consideration this menace and had installed certain fire-fighting apparatus.

In order that this might be used to the best advantage, Tom had instructed his men in a fire drill, similar to that used on ships at sea when the call to fire quarters is sounded at unexpected intervals to accustom the passengers to acting sanely in times of excitement.

Now, as Eradicate's warning cry sounded forth, Tom did not lose his head, but at once pulled the level of the automatic signal which informed those in the plane above, as well as those in the car, that they must prepare to fight for their lives.

"Put on the parachutes!" Tom cried, for there was one of these life-savers for every person on board. As you know, all the mail-plane fliers now wear these "umbrellas," as do all army fliers. The parachute is made from a particular kind of raw silk cloth. It can be folded into a very small compass, and is strapped around a flier's body by means of leather belts going around his legs and waist. On the waist belt is an iron ring, and as the person jumps from a burning plane, or one that is crippled and falling, this iron ring is pulled.

Immediately it releases the cords that hold the parachute in folds and the silk spreads out in the form of an immense umbrella. The air, getting under this, acts as a brake, and the person comes to the ground much more gently than otherwise would be the case. Even with the parachutes, however, there is danger in the fall, if it happens to be in a tree, and often there is peril in falling into the water. But, with all those, there is much more chance for life than if none is used. There is, too, always the danger that the parachute will not open in time, but this happens so rarely that it need not be considered.

"Bless my door mat!" cried Mr. Damon,

fumbling with the straps. "I hope I don't get this thing on backward!"

"This is the way it goes!" cried Ned, who already had his adjusted.

Tom, likewise, had adjusted his safety device, and now the young inventor, thinking regretfully meanwhile of this sudden ending of his hopes, began to prepare for "abandoning ship."

"Come here, Rad!" he called, for though the colored man's voice had issued from the galley with the warning cry of fire, the man himself had not appeared. "Hurry, Rad!" cried Tom.

A moment later his old servant showed himself.

"What happened, Rad?" cried Tom. "Quick! Is the kitchen on fire? The automatic chemical sprinkler ought to have worked!"

"No, Massa Tom," answered the old colored man. "De kitchen didn't cotch fire—jes' dis pie whut I was makin' fo' yo'. I put her in de oven ob de gaskoliny stove, and den I forgot it. 'Case why? 'Case dat big giant got hungry an' wanted me to fix him up suffin to eat. An' when I were doin' dat mah pie burned! Look, it's laik a piece ob charcoal."

"And do you mean to tell me, Rad, that you raised an alarm of fire just because a pie burned?" cried Tom, somewhat sternly.

"Suah, I did," was the answer. "Why not? It was a fine pie!"

"Well, bless my insurance policy!" exclaimed Mr. Damon while the others stood listening, hardly knowing whether to laugh or not. "You sure did give us a scare, Rad!"

"I should say so!" murmured Tom. "Whew, but I'm glad it wasn't true! It would have meant the end of my hopes. Mr. Jacks wouldn't invest any more money if we burned up on the second third of our trip. But are you sure everything's all right, Rad?"

"Yes, Massa Tom, eberyt'ing but dish yeah pie!" and ruefully the old colored fellow held out the remains of the pastry.

"Well, I'm glad it was no worse," replied the young inventor. "I guess we can take these off," he went on, as he began loosening his parachute belt. The others did likewise, and then word was relayed to the mechanicians in the plane above that all was well and that there was no need to leap out.

"Well, then we'll descend on Denver in the way we originally intended," decided Tom, for they were now over that interesting and historic city.

The same scenes were enacted here as had taken place in Chicago. A big crowd was on hand to welcome and cheer Tom Swift and his comrades, and the natural western exuberance of the people was a little too much for the police. Tom had difficulty in piloting the unclamped car through the mass of curious ones to the waiting *Osprey*, the propellers of which were slowly whirring in anticipation of the flight to the Pacific coast.

But after answering many questions of the reporters and posing for his photograph and for the movie men, Tom at last was in the car beneath the third aeroplane. It was now well on in the afternoon, and if the originator of the airline express hoped to do the entire distance in sixteen hours it behooved him to "get a hustle on," as Ned expressed it.

"The hardest part of the trip is ahead of us. Tom," his manager said.

"I know it is," was the answer. "Over the Rockies. But the predicted storm hasn't come to the scratch, and I'm glad of that. It means quite a gain in time not to run into bad weather."

"Better wait before you crow," said Ned. "We have about six hours of riding ahead of us, and there's no telling what we may meet with."

Tom was glad to note, by inspections of the various gages, that the *Osprey* was doing better in regard to speed than either the *Falcon* or the *Eagle*. She fairly roared and soared her way into the air after leaving Denver, carrying aloft, in the car beneath her, the young inventor and his friends.

Tom got the wireless apparatus to working and

after some difficulty succeeded in establishing communication with his home, where he talked to Mrs. Baggert.

"Your father is lying down, taking a nap," reported the housekeeper. "Yes, he's all right. But a queer message came in over the local office telephone a little while ago, Tom. Wait, I'll repeat it to you. I answered, because no one else was around, and I heard a voice saying: 'Tell Tom Swift not to count his chickens before they're hatched!' And then a man's voice laughed. I tried to find out who it was and where the message came from, but I couldn't."

"Oh, well, don't worry about it," Tom advised Mrs. Baggert, though he himself felt not a little anxious. "They're still up to their old tricks, Ned," Tom reported to his financial manager.

"Well, they can't get at us while we're up here," Ned answered.

"No, but we aren't at San Francisco yet, and something may happen there," Tom replied. "I do hope they won't make any more trouble for Dad."

"He will be well looked after by Mrs. Baggert and the others," was Ned's consoling reply.

On and on roared the *Osprey*, like the great hawk whose name she bore, winging her way toward the great open space of the Pacific. The hours rolled around, and they were crossing a wild and desolate rocky region when suddenly the comparative stillness was broken by a loud, booming sound, as if of an explosion.

"What's that?" exclaimed Ned, and Tom, who was making a log record of the trip, looked up apprehensively.

"Thunder!" answered Mr. Damon, who was sitting near one of the observation windows. "I just saw a flash of lightning. I guess we're running into a storm."

There was no doubt of it a few moments later. With the *Osprey* rushing forward and the mountain storm coming to meet the craft, it was only a short time before the airline express was in the midst of a violent outburst of the elements.

"Whew, this is fierce!" cried Tom, as there came a blinding flash, followed by a terrific clap, and then, almost immediately after, by a shower of rain as if a cloud had burst above them.

CHAPTER XXI

THE GOLDEN GATE

CAUGHT in the very center of a fierce mountain storm, the *Osprey* was now battling her way above the jagged and towering peaks of the Rockies, fighting for every inch in an endeavor to reach San Francisco within the stipulated time. Though by the clock there were several hours of daylight still remaining, it was so dark and gloomy in the stormy mountain region that it seemed as if night had fallen.

"But we may pull out of it yet!" cried Tom to his friends, as he saw to it that all the openings of the traveling car were tightly closed. For once the air, under high pressure because of the velocity of the wind, gained an entrance, it might do serious damage. But Tom had foreseen that they might run into storms, and had so built his car that a few pulls on certain levers would close everything save the protected ventilators.

Through these fresh air came in and the foul air was expelled, but rain could not enter. It

169

was different in the aeroplane above the car, how-ever. There the mechanician and his assistant were pretty much in the open, though there was a cowl of heavy celluloid to protect their faces and Tom had rigged up an extra hood to keep off some of the rain and snow that might be en-countered on the trip. But from the very nature of their calling, aeroplane pilots must fly with much of their bodies exposed to the elements.

When they expect to go to great heights and encounter cold of such intensity that it is hard to conceive of it, they wear suits in which are woven wires of high resistance. A low voltage electric current, passing through these wires, warms them, just as is done in some of the warming pads used in bed by invalids. In this way the blood of the daring aviators is kept circulating.

But as Tom did not expect to go very high on his airline express trips, there was no need of these electrically heated suits, and none had been taken along. However, he had taken into considera-tion that they might run into rain, and rubber coats had been provided.

"I'll go up and relieve Ted Dolan," remarked Tom to Ned, for the third crew of pilots had been taken on at Denver to make the final hop to the Pacific coast. Dolan was an experienced airman and had for his helper Art Wright. But they had not taken their rubber coats up in the cockpit with them, for when they left Denver the weather was all that could be desired.

"I'll go with you," offered Ned. "I'd like to see just how bad this storm is."

"It's a humdinger all right," declared Tom, as he glanced out of an observation window while waiting for Eradicate to bring the storm garments from a locker.

"Bless my nose-guard, I'll say it is!" chimed in Mr. Damon. "I never saw a worse one."

"Oh, we've been in just as severe ones before," observed Tom, in what seemed a cool voice. "When we were trying out the flying boat I remember a storm when I thought we never would get through it. This is bad enough, but the *Osprey* can buck it I think."

"Ah knows Massa Tom gwine to pull us through all right," said Eradicate, with a glance at Koku. "Ah isn't scairt, no how!"

"Huh! Black man talk big—but him knees shake all same," sneered the giant.

"Whose knees am shakin', big man? Whose knees am shakin'?" demanded the colored servant, as he strode toward the big fellow. It seemed as if he might try to punch Koku.

"That will do," commanded Tom in a low voice. He had troubles enough on hand without a fight starting between his two helpers.

A signal was given for Wright to descend to

the cabin, and when he came down Tom went up through the enclosed ladder.

"Is it bad up there?" he asked his workman.

"Bad?" was the reply. "Say, you ought to feel it!" He was wet through—as dripping as though he had fallen into a tub of water.

When Tom took charge of the cockpit Dolan descended, glad enough to get out of the way of the stinging pellets of rain, driven by the hurricane wind. He, too, was soaked. Ned followed his chum up into the cockpit, and, though they were protected by goggles, helmets of leather, and rubber coats, they felt the force of the storm.

What with the roaring of the motors, the howl of the wind, the crash of thunder, and the rattle of the rain, it was impossible for the two to communicate, even though they had speaking tubes running from the forward cockpit to the one built aft.

The young inventor, who had taken personal charge of piloting the big plane through the storm, that it might arrive on time, soon realized that he had his "work cut out for him," as he said later. While it is not at all unusual for aeroplanes of even less power than the big ones Tom used to fly through storms, still there is always the element of danger.

thusiasm. "But do you think you'll lose all of two hours, Tom?"

"Fully that," Tom admitted, rather ruefully. "I did hope we might make it in sixteen hours and a few minutes, as I said we could do. But that storm actually cut two hours, if not more, off our schedule. However, it can't be helped."

So rapidly was the *Osprey* making time now that it seemed as if the Golden Gate were rushing forward and opening wide to receive the wonderful craft and her occupants. It is the sun, setting in a glory of gold outside the harbor of San Francisco that gives the poetical name to the city, as much so, perhaps, as the yellow nuggets it produced in the days that never will return.

There came a signal from the car. It was Ted Dolan calling up to Tom:

"Do you want to be relieved?"

"Thank you, no," the young inventor answered. "I'll stick now and make the landing."

"I thought you might want to do so," Ted said. "But if the storm played you out, Art and I will take her for a little while and you and Mr. Newton can come up again just before making the landing."

"No, I'll stick," announced Tom. "How about you?" he asked his chum.

"I'm game, of course. I wouldn't miss it for

anything. They ought to reward you publicly in some way, Tom!"

"Reward! What for?"

"For establishing this airline express—crossing the United States in the daylight hours of a single day."

"Reward nothing! If I can do it, the only reward I want is for Jason Jacks and others who can afford it to invest money in the project and get it firmly established."

"Oh, they'll do that all right, Tom. Is that the landing field below us?"

Ned pointed to a green level stretch outside the city of San Francisco. They had approached it rapidly, for the *Osprey*, as if determining to live up to her name, was fairly zooming toward the Pacific.

"That's it," was the answer. "There's quite a crowd there, too! Hope I don't muss anybody's hair as I go down. Confound the people! Why don't they know enough to keep out of the way when they see an aeroplane coming down right among 'em?"

Well might Tom ask this, for the crowd, which had assembled in anticipation of seeing the landing, was swarming all over the field in spite of the efforts of the police to keep a free place for the machine to come down.

"I'll give 'em a bit of a scare," decided Tom.

Quickly shifting the rudder of his plane, it appeared for a moment as if he was going to crash down where the crowd was thickest. With yells of alarm the people scattered, and this left a clear space, which was what Tom wanted.

"Now for a landing, Ned!" he called to his chum. "Mark the time!"

"Mark it is!" answered Ned, who sat with his watch in one hand and a pencil in the other, ready to make the record on the official slip of paper he held on his knee. "It's over eighteen hours, though, Tom," he said regretfully.

"I'm afraid it is, Ned. But it can't be helped, Better luck next time!"

"Hope so," was the response.

A moment later, amid the wild and enthusiastic cheers of the crowd, Tom brought the *Osprey* to earth, the first time she had touched it since leaving Denver. The car landed with a gentle thud, rolled along a little way and then came to a stop while the crowd of reporters, cameramen, and general curiosity seekers rushed forward in an overwhelming wave. It was a reproduction of the same scenes that had taken place in Chicago and Denver, only this was more intensified, for it marked the end of the journey.

But before Tom would reply to the score of questions hurled at him by the reporters he called to Ned:

"What time do you make it?"

The manager figured rapidly.

"Eighteen hours and sixteen minutes from Long Island to San Francisco," he answered.

"Not so bad," murmured Tom. "But we're going to do better than that the next time."

And then, as he stepped down from the plane, he was surrounded by an excited and curious crowd.

"Tell us about it! What was the exact running time? Did you have any accidents? How do you feel? When are you going to make the return trip?"

These, and dozens of other questions, were fairly volleyed at Tom by the newspaper men, and he answered as best he could. By this time he was used to the printed publicity that followed his work, and he knew the value of it. So he was always courteous and kind to the reporters and photographers, patiently posing for the latter and letting them take as many pictures as they wanted.

It was a great feat, and every one realized that. As soon as enterprising reporters had telephoned the facts in to their papers in San Francisco, whistles were blown and bells were rung to celebrate the event. Tom was a popular hero, much as he disliked the rôle.

The news of his arrival was flashed back over

land wires and by means of radio to New York and the East, though Tom did not wait for Mary and his father to receive the good news in this indirect way. As soon as he had given the reporters the gist of the story, speaking of the terrible storm through which they had run, Tom had his operator get in touch with his home on the radio. In a short time Tom's voice was heard in the house at Shopton where Mary, her father and mother, and Mr. Swift had been sitting, anxiously waiting. It was night there, though still daylight in San Francisco.

"I'm all right, Dad!" reported the young inventor. "Didn't make it quite as speedily as I hoped, but I'll do better on the return trip. How's Mary?"

"She's all right," answered Mr. Swift. "She will speak to you in a moment. But, Tom, be careful. I'm worried about you. A number of mysterious messages have come in over the telephone wires during the day. I'm afraid your enemies are still on your trail."

"Well, maybe they are, Dad, but I think I have given them the slip," laughed Tom. "Anyhow, they couldn't stop me from making this one trip. And now let me talk to Mary."

They were soon in conversation and the girl was greatly relieved to learn that Tom and his friends were safe.

"But do be careful, won't you?" she begged.

"I sure will!" Tom promised. "Don't worry! I haven't seen any of those fellows out here. Guess it was too far for them."

He was soon to learn, however, that this was not the case.

Bidding Mary good-bye over the radio and promising to talk to her again as soon as he could, Tom shut off the power on the wireless and made preparations for having his machine guarded during the night. Except for some of the mechanicians who would sleep on board, the others were to go to a hotel. There they would get some much-needed rest and prepare to make the return trip in a few days. Tom wanted time, however, to have the engines carefully gone over. Also he wanted to communicate with the crews in Denver and Chicago and have them alert and ready to speed him on his way when the return trip should be made.

A hasty inspection of the *Osprey* showed that the plane had sustained no damage in flying through the storm, but could, after a few adjustments, make the return journey.

"Well, what do you say to a good bath, Ned, and a lobster supper?" asked Tom of his chum, when they had summoned an automobile which would take them and Mr. Damon, with Eradicate, to the hotel.

"That sounds good to me," Ned answered.

"Koku he stay and guard machine," announced the big giant proudly, for Tom had informed him that was to be his duty.

"Don't let anybody near it," cautioned his master.

"Anybody come—Koku make 'um all full holes," was the grim answer.

"Mebby Ah better stay, too," suggested Eradicate.

"No, I want you with me, Rad," Tom said. "I need looking after and so does Ned. We brought only one suit of clothes each, and they need pressing."

"Dat's whut I'll do!" said the old colored man. He was pleased thus to serve his master.

So great was the interest manifested by the papers in Tom's exploit that he could hardly get away from the reporters long enough to eat. At last he had fairly to beg them to give him a few minutes of quiet, and reluctantly they consented.

But after he had bathed and dined they were at him again, so it was long past midnight when Tom was really free. Mr. Damon, tired with the unusual trip, had retired, and thus Tom and his financial manager found themselves left pretty much alone.

"I don't feel a bit like sleeping," Tom said, "I'd only toss and tumble if I went to bed."

"Same here," agreed Ned.

"What do you say if we take a run out to the plane?" asked Tom. "I'd like to make sure she's all right, even with Koku and the others on guard. There's altogether too much curiosity about her."

"I'm with you—come on."

A taxicab took them out to the landing field, but, being a new man, the driver made a wrong approach and found himself on a blind road, half a mile from the *Osprey's* landing place.

"Never mind," said Tom, when the man offered to go back and approach by the proper route. "We can make better time by walking across lots. This will do."

Tom paid and dismissed the driver and then he and Ned made their way through the darkness, somewhat illuminated by the moon, toward the place where the craft rested. Their approach was unnoticed, which was beginning to make Tom think that perhaps Koku was not as active on guard duty as he might have been, when suddenly from the bushes just ahead of them a man sprang. He started to run away, but Ned, sensing something suspicious in his movements, sprang forward and caught hold of him.

"Who are you?" cried the young financial

manager. "What have you been doing? Show
a light here, Tom," for Ned knew his chum carried a pocket flashlight.

When the gleam was thrown on the man's
face Tom cried:

"Kenny! You here!"

Then, to the surprise of Tom and Ned, the
fellow broke down and actually began to whim-
per as if his spirit was broken.

"I give up, Mr. Swift!" he exclaimed. "I
can't fight against you! It's too big a thing
you've done. Nobody else could have done it.
I'm through with those fellows! But look out
—they'll ruin you if they get the chance. Now
have me arrested if you want to—I'm done!"

He stood there, making no effort to escape,
a broken, dejected man.

CHAPTER XXIII

ANOTHER CAPTURE

Tom Swift could not understand this attitude on the part of Kenny. The fellow had been one of the four (including the two mysterious masked men) who had captured Tom in the tunnel and had held him a prisoner on the island in the lake. Kenny had seemed as relentless and vicious as any of the four who were intent on getting away from Tom his patent on the airline express.

Now, after an easy capture, Kenny had broken down—given up—and professed to be sorry. It did not seem natural. No wonder Tom and Ned were on their guard.

"What were you doing back there at the plane, if that's where you were?" demanded Tom, while Ned held the prisoner fast.

"Yes, I was near your plane, but I didn't do any damage—I—I just couldn't," Kenny faltered.

"Were you going to do any damage?" Tom inquired sternly.

"I was—if I could—yes," was the reply. "They wanted me to blow it up or damage it in some way, so you couldn't make the return trip. But I hadn't the heart to do it—I just couldn't bring myself to it, Mr. Swift—I just couldn't."

"Who do you mean wanted you to blow up my machine?" asked the young inventor. "Was it Schlump and those two masked men? Who are they, anyhow?"

"Yes, it was them. But I can't tell you who those other two are," was the reply. "It would mean death to me if I squealed. But I'm through. Do what you like with me, only don't let those fellows get hold of me. I'm done for if you do."

"How do you know but what you aren't done for now?" asked Ned grimly. "We've got you fast, and your confession is enough to send you to jail. Kidnapping is a serious crime, you know."

"I don't mind going to jail," whimpered Kenny. "That would be better than being killed—never knowing when the blow was going to fall. If I'm in jail they can't get me. And they'll try to, for they'll soon know I didn't carry out my end of the bargain."

"Well, you're going to jail all right!" declared Tom. "It may be the best and safest place for you, and I surely will feel better when you're behind bars. But what's the game, anyhow? Why should Schlump and those two masked men want to do me harm?"

"I can't tell you," Kenny faltered. "I have betrayed them enough as it is, and I'm not going to say any more. I give up—that's enough for you—and I warn you to look out. Now all I want is protection from them. Have me locked up; I deserve it."

This Tom and Ned had decided at once to do. But they were still suspicious over Kenny's sudden breakdown after his capture. That might be a plot to throw them off the track, to enable the other plotters to get in their work. Tom resolved to be on his guard.

Koku and some of the others in the plane car had come out on hearing voices, and in a few words the young inventor explained what had happened.

"I keep him," said Koku significantly, as he took hold of Kenny.

"Don't let him kill me!" pleaded the prisoner.

"He won't hurt you—that is, if you don't try to get away," said Tom grimly.

"I'm not going to. I'm through, I tell you.' Why, if I had wanted to I could have blown you to pieces half an hour ago. Go over there and look!" he exclaimed, pointing to a spot near some empty boxes and cases, that had contained materials used in preparing the landing field.

"Take a look, Ned," suggested Tom, handing his chum the flashlight.

In a few minutes Ned came back bearing an object, at the sight of which some of the workmen cried:

"It's a bomb! Look out!"

"The firing apparatus has been taken out—here it is," said Kenny, and he took something from his pocket. "It can't go off the way it is," he added.

A quick inspection on the part of Tom proved the truth of this. A bomb had been concealed in the rubbish, and, had it gone off, it very likely would have wrecked the *Osprey*, and, possibly, have injured or killed those in the car.

"But I couldn't do it," confessed Kenny. "I had it all ready to plant and was going to set the time fuse when I weakened."

"Why did you do that?" asked Tom, still suspicious.

"To tell you the truth, it was because I couldn't bear to wreck such a fine machine as you have made," Kenny admitted, and there was a bit of pride in his voice and look. "I'm a good mechanic," he went on. "You found that out in the shop before I was discharged, didn't you?" he asked.

"Yes, you were an expert in your line," admitted Tom.

"Well, I got in bad company—maybe that's how you can account for it," proceeded Kenny. "I'm not defending myself—but I got in wrong and bad. You did right to fire me—but then I wanted my revenge. I was in the crowd that saw you come down to-day," he told Tom. "The gang sent me on here to finish the job which they couldn't do in Shopton because you were too well guarded. They figured it would be easier here, and it was. I didn't have much trouble hiding that bomb.

"But when I saw you come sailing in and knew you had almost done the journey as you said you'd do it—in sixteen hours—I just didn't have the heart to destroy the machine. It would be like a man running his pet auto into a stone wall deliberately. I didn't have the heart. You needn't believe me, but that's the truth."

"I do believe you—in that, at least," Tom said. Being a mechanic himself he could understand another workman's love for a wonderful piece of machinery. "But that doesn't let you out, Kenny," said Tom sternly.

"I know it doesn't, Mr. Swift. "I'm not asking to be let off. I'm better in jail as it is. I don't want those fellows to get me, for they'll know I double-crossed 'em. Lock me up—that's all I ask. I'm down and out!"

He really seemed so, and was as honest as he could be under the circumstances. Strange as it may appear, his love for machinery in the abstract, his delight in a perfect piece of work, had overcome his promise to his confederates. Tom believed this much of his story.

The police were notified and Kenny was taken to jail, on the technical charge, in lieu of another, of unlawfully possessing explosives. For the time fuse found on him contained a charge heavy enough in itself to have done considerable damage.

"Well, that's one out of the way," commented Tom to Ned after Kenny had been taken off.

"Yes. But there are three left, according to his talk, and maybe more," said the manager. "What are you going to do about them?"

"I'm going to carry on—fly back to New York Tuesday," was the answer. "But at the same time I'll be on the watch. It is hardly possible that any more of the gang are out here. They depended on Kenny, and he double-crossed them, to our advantage. And they won't have time to start anything at Denver or Chicago— they can't get there in time. They'll know, of course, by watching the papers, that nothing happened to us here. They can argue either that Kenny failed or threw them down—it doesn't matter which they decide on. But their next move will be made at the Long Island field—if they move at all."

And, thinking it over, Ned came to the same conclusion.

Accordingly preparations were made for the return trip of the *Osprey* to Denver where the *Eagle* would pick up the car and carry it to Chicago.

There were enthusiastic scenes as Tom hopped off early Tuesday morning, when it was hardly daylight. He had sent a message the night before to Mary and his father, telling them of the start.

Tom's trip back to the East was even more successful than his trip out, and he made better flying time by the hour, for no storm was encountered. The same wild scenes of greeting when he landed in Denver and Chicago were witnessed again, and word of his progress was flashed by wireless and telegraph as he passed over city after city on his way home.

In due time he reached the landing field in Long Island and received a roaring welcome. The first round trip had been made successfully, and but five more remained to be made before the rich Mr. Jacks would put in enough money to insure the financial success of the new enterprise. And once it became known that Jacks had invested others would do the same, Tom reasoned.

So it was with a feeling of pride and satisfaction that Tom went back to Shopton to tell his father and Mary all the details. He decided to let a week elapse before trying another journey, as there were some mechanical changes he wanted to make in the car.

Then came the second round trip, the time being cut down a little, but not enough to satisfy Tom.

On the third one he was so long delayed by a storm that his time was a half hour more than on his first trip west. However, he was still within the daylight stipulation, and Mr. Jacks announced himself satisfied thus far.

"Three more round trips, and I'll come in on a big scale," said the old millionaire. "It begins to look feasible, Tom Swift."

"It is feasible, Mr. Jacks," was the answer. "You'll see!"

However, the millionaire came very near not "seeing," for the night before the sixth round trip was to start something ominous happened out at the Long Island hangar.

Tom and his friends had gone to a hotel there, to be in readiness for an early morning start. The young inventor had inspected the machinery and found everything in perfect order.

Koku and Eradicate had been left on guard, their differences for a time being patched up. Each one was proud of his part in the night's work.

It was shortly after midnight when Eradicate, carefully marching around his end of the plane, thought he detected a movement in the bushes. The old man's eyesight was none of the best, much as he disliked to admit this, but he decided he would do better to summon Koku, which he did.

"Maybe dere's somebody ober dere, big man," whispered Eradicate, pointing.

The giant was like a cat—he could see in the dark. For a moment he bent his gaze on the bush indicated by the colored man. Then with a roar of anger the big fellow rushed forward, jumped into the shrubbery and came out, dragging after him a struggling man.

"Let me go! Let me go!" cried this individual. He tried to get something out of his pocket, but Koku held his hand until other watchmen came with lights, and then it was seen that the prisoner was Schlump. An ugly sight he was, too, his face inflamed with rage. Koku pulled his hand from the pocket and found that Schlump was clutching a deadly bomb with a time fuse which shortly would have set it off. But some of the mechanics soon rendered the infernal machine harmless, and Schlump was taken before Tom.

"So, we've caught you, have we?" asked the young inventor.

"So it seems!" Schlump snarled. "But you'd better try to save yourself! The others are still after you! I'm not the only one! And you haven't got me yet—not quite!"

With an unexpected and quick motion he broke away from Koku and ran off in the darkness.

CHAPTER XXIV

TROUBLES AND WORRIES

INSTANTLY the scene just outside the hangar where the plane and the car were kept was in confusion. So quickly had Schlump given his captor the slip that, for a moment, every one was stunned. Even Tom Swift, accustomed as he was to emergencies, did not know what to do. But this hesitation was only momentary.

"Get him!" shouted the young inventor. "We've got to get him! Scatter and round him up!"

"Turn on the searchlight!" yelled Ned.

"By golly!" chuckled Eradicate, who had seen the man get away from the giant, "dat big man ain't so smart whut he t'ink he am."

"Never mind that now, Rad!" ordered Tom, a bit sternly. "Forget your fights with Koku and see if you can find this fellow! We want to question him and see if we can't get on the trail of the masked men and others who are trying to queer my plans!"

"Yes, sah," humbly answered the colored man. "I'll cotch him!"

But this was more easily said than done. Though the big searchlight was flashed on, its beams crossing and recrossing the field about the hangar like a giant's finger, the plotter was not picked up. The chances were greatly in his favor, running off in the darkness as he had, and after an hour's search it became evident that he was not to be caught.

"Come back," Tom advised his friends and the workmen. "We'll have to let him go," he added, as they made their way back to their temporary headquarters. "We got the bomb away from him, and we'll take care that he doesn't approach near enough the remainder of the night to plant another. We'll have to organize a patrol, Ned."

"I guess that's right," assented the financial manager. "We can't take any chances."

Reluctantly Koku gave up the search, for he felt it was his fault that Schlump had escaped.

"Nex' time I sot on him!" declared the giant.

"He'll be like a pancake when you get up," chuckled Ned.

The rest of the night every precaution was taken to prevent any damage being done to the plane or the car. Men walked about the hangar in relays, and the slightest suspicious object or movement was at once investigated. Nothing happened, and when the first glimmer of dawn appeared, Tom made ready to hop off on what he hoped would be the last trip before he would fulfil the conditions of Jason Jacks.

"Those fellows must know that everything depends on my completion of the six round trips, Ned," said the young inventor as he took his place in the car, while Meldrum and Dodge went to the cockpit of the aeroplane. "They think if they can put me out of business I won't get the money to complete the patent work and establish the line as a practical concern."

"I suppose so," agreed Ned. "But how do you think they know that?"

"Oh, there has been a lot of talk over the financing of this thing. You know that," remarked Tom. "It isn't extraordinary that some of these plotters would get to hear about it. I wish we could have held on to Schlump, though."

"So do I! He might have given information that would help us catch those other two—the ones you say wore masks. I wonder who they could be?"

"I have an idea," said Tom. "I'll tell you later if my suspicions are correct. But now we've got to get busy. I'm going to try to break the time record this trip. If I do it will please the old millionaire. Then, when we come back from San Francisco—if we do—and make it somewhere near the sixteen hours, he'll put in the rest of the cash."

"And believe me, we'll need it!" exclaimed Ned, in such fervent tones that Tom asked:

"Why, is our bank balance low?"

"Well, it isn't anything to boast of," Ned answered. "You know we had to dip into it pretty heavily to finance this thing—not only in building the planes but in securing the landing fields and paying the men who look after them."

"Yes, it has taken a bit of money," admitted Tom. "But then, after we are successful, and I'm sure we shall be, we'll get it all back, and more, too."

"Yes," agreed Ned. "Well, let's go!"

He followed Ned and the others into the main compartment of the car which had been clamped to the aeroplane in readiness for the start. Though Ned did not tell Tom, the finances of the Swifts were in a very precarious state just then. Of course the firm owned much property and many valuable patents, but the Swift Construction Company had drawn largely on its credit, borrowing from the banks, and to raise more cash meant the stretching of the credit to a danger point. By selling some of their holdings, cash could have been raised, certainly; but no business man likes to sacrifice any of his principle, and Ned was a good business man.

In order to keep the airline going, Ned had been forced to use some of his own money which he had saved, though he did not tell Tom this for fear it would worry him. And then, when it was found that more cash was needed, Ned had spoken of the matter to Mary Nestor, having already gotten all Mr. Damon could spare.

"Take all I have!" exclaimed the girl. "I'm glad to invest it in anything Tom has to do with."

"No, we won't take it all," Ned had replied. He knew she had quite a large sum that she had inherited from her grandmother, and it was in her own name. "But if you could lend a few thousands and not worry if it was lost for a time, we could use it nicely."

"Take it!" generously offered Mary. "But what do you mean about being lost for a time?"

"I mean that even if this airline express project fails in the present instance," replied Ned, "that Tom will eventually succeed with it and pay off his debts."

"Of course he will!" said Mary proudly.

"And even if this is a complete failure," went on Ned, "and we must, as a business proposition, take that into consideration, Tom will start something else that will pay big and he'll get back all he loses on this. So it isn't as if I were asking you to throw your money away."

"Take all I have!" exclaimed Mary impulsively.

But Ned was content with a comparatively small sum. And it was on this money and some of his own, together with what remained from the original sale of stock, that the last two trips were financed. If they failed—well, Ned did not like to think of that.

So in blissful ignorance of the sword of failure that was hanging over his head, suspended, as it were, on a thin thread of dollar bills, Tom prepared to make this last trip.

It was hardly daylight when they hopped off, careful watch being kept by the men at the hangar lest, in the last moment, Schlump might slip up and toss a bomb that would kill, injure, and destroy. But nothing untoward happened, and soon the plane and its accompanying car was speeding away over the New Jersey meadows while behind the travelers the east grew lighter and lighter as the sun slowly mounted in the heavens.

Aside from the anxiety of all on board to make the best time possible on this trip, nothing unusual occurred during the first lap. Tom had to stop a quarrel between Eradicate and Koku, for the colored man could not refrain from taunting the giant over letting Schlump get away. So infuriated did the big man become under the taunts of Eradicate that he might have done the latter an injury had not Tom sternly forbidden all further mention of the incident.

Chicago was reached safely, almost half an hour ahead of the schedule, which fact, when Tom ascertained it, made him exclaim:

"Fine! If we can keep that up we'll do better than sixteen hours to the coast. We're going to push the motors for all they're capable of from now on."

"Better not strain 'em too much, sir," suggested Sam Stone, who was to pilot the *Eagle* part of the way on the second lap. "We don't want to break anything."

"No," said Tom, "we don't want to break anything but records. How has everything been here? Any signs of those rascals?"

"Well, there have been one or two suspicious fellows loitering around the hangar," reported the mechanician. "But we warned them away. They didn't blow us up, at any rate."

"I'm glad of that," said Tom. "They tried it on Long Island," and he related the Schlump incident. "He'll probably wire his confederates out here or in Denver or San Francisco to muss us up if they can—anything to prevent this last trip from succeeding. So we must redouble our precautions."

"We'll do that," agreed Stone.

The *Eagle* at first did even better than the *Falcon*, and it seemed as if the hop between Chicago and Denver would be a record-breaker. But slight trouble developed about halfway across the plains, and though it was remedied, still they were forty minutes late, which not only ate up the half hour they had gained on the first lap, but cut ten minutes from the remaining time.

"But we'll make it up on the last lap!" declared Tom, with confidence. "Push her for all she's got in her, boys!" he said to Dolan and Wright, who climbed into the cockpit at Denver.

They got off to a roaring start, rose high in the air, and then headed straight for the Golden Gate.

"I sure will be glad when the last trip is over," remarked Mr. Damon, who sat in the car near Tom and Ned.

"Why, are you getting tired of it?" asked the young inventor.

"No. But my wife doesn't speak to me, and

she says she won't as long as I take these crazy air trips. But I said I'd come on the last trip with you, Tom, and I'm going to stick!"

"Well, I hope you don't drop out now," grimly joked Ned, as he looked from an observation window to the earth, several thousand feet below.

"Bless my feather bed, I should hope not!" cried the odd man.

Tom kept note of the distance traveled and the time used, and as several hours passed and the figures grew a pleased smile came over his face.

"It begins to look as if we'd make up all we lost and more too, Ned!" he cried to his chum.

The whistle of the tube communicating from the car to the cockpit sent out a shrill summons

"Hello! What is it?" called Tom.

"You'd better come up here, Mr. Swift," answered the voice of Art Wright. "Dolan seems to be knocked out and the motor is behaving very queerly. I'm afraid it's going to die on us!"

CHAPTER XXV

A GLORIOUS FINISH

"Stand by, Ned!" ordered Tom, in a low voice. "Get ready to follow me up above," and the young inventor made ready to ascend the enclosed ladder to the cockpit overhead.

"What's wrong?" asked Ned.

"I don't know; but it looks like dirty work. I'm afraid they've got us, after all!"

"How could they?"

Tom did not stop to answer, but quickly ascended the ladder. Ned, in a few words, told the others the alarming news that had come down from the cockpit, and then stood ready to carry out Tom's orders.

The young inventor, crowding into the narrow space of the after cockpit, found Wright managing the machinery, for the planes had a dual control system. In the forward cockpit Ted Dolan was slumped down in a heap.

"What's the matter?" cried Tom, when he reached Dolan's side.

"I don't know," the mechanician answered

weakly. "It's something I ate—or else I've been doped. My stomach seems caved in and I can't see. I'll have to quit, Mr. Swift—sorry——"

"Don't worry about that!" exclaimed Tom. "Ned and I can finish the trip—if the engine's all right."

"But that's just the trouble," went on Dolan, in a weak voice. "She isn't acting properly."

"Seems to be some obstruction in the oil feed line," said Wright.

"Use the other," Tom promptly advised.

"They're both feeding slowly," was the answer. "If the oil stops, we stop too!" Tom well knew that.

"You get down to the cabin, Dolan," advised the young inventor. "Mr. Damon will look after you—he's a traveling medicine chest. But have you been eating or drinking with strangers?"

"Nothing like that, Mr. Swift—no, sir! I only ate meals I was sure of, and at the hangar too. I never drank anything but water—not even sodas, for I know they can knock you out in hot weather. I think somebody got in the hangar and doped my food."

"It's possible," admitted Tom. "How about you?" he asked the assistant.

"I'm all right—I can stick."

"Well, we may need you later. You go down now with Dolan and look after him, and send Mr. Newton up here."

Having given these orders, Tom began looking over the machinery. He was engaged in this when Ned came up to help, reporting that Mr. Damon was looking after the ill mechanician.

"What's wrong?" asked Ned.

"Oil feed supply," was the short answer. "You run the plane, Ned, and I'll take the pipe down and clean it. We can run on one line while I'm working on the other."

It was a few minutes later, when Tom had the pipe uncoupled, that he uttered an exclamation of anger and surprise.

"What is it?" cried Ned.

Tom held out a piece of cork. It had been stuffed into the pipe in such a way that for a time enough oil would pass to keep the motors running, but the cork would gradually swell and eventually would completely clog the pipe, shutting off all oil.

Without oil an engine will soon heat up, until, because of friction, the bearings, slide rods, pistons and cylinder walls may become red-hot. When that occurs the engine naturally stops. And when the engine of an aeroplane stops the plane falls. It is not like a dirigible that can sustain itself.

"Dirty work!" bitterly murmured Tom, as he worked with all possible speed to replace the pipe, for the secondary oil supply was fast failing. The plane was losing speed rapidly.

"Somebody must have got in, put some sort of dope in Dolan's food or water, and also clogged the pipes," said Ned.

"Right!" snapped out Tom. "But we aren't beaten yet!"

And they were not. By hard work the young inventor got the other oil line cleaned, and then the *Osprey* at once picked up speed. However, much valuable time had been lost, and Tom was anxious lest the motors might have been permanently damaged by running without sufficient oil.

But they must carry on now, at all hazards, for they were within striking distance of their goal. They at last settled down into the San Francisco landing field after dark—a poor record, nearly twenty hours having been consumed since starting.

"Lucky I'm not on a strict time limit for these six trips," commented Tom as, tired and exhausted from work and worry, he climbed out of the cockpit, followed by Ned. "Jacks didn't stipulate that we must keep to the sixteen-hour schedule for these six trips. His only condition was that we must fly continually from coast to coast, with landings only at Chicago and Denver, and we've done that."

"Through good luck and management," commented Ned. "But we've got to be mighty careful, Tom, on the last trip back. They'll be out to do us if they can and spoil our chances of getting that hundred thousand dollars from Jacks."

"You said it! Well, we'll do the best we can."

Extraordinary precautions were taken about the hangar that night. Men continually patrolled the place, and even newspaper reporters and photographers were looked upon with suspicion. None but those with unquestionable credentials were allowed within the enclosure.

Tom had intended starting back to New York about three days after his arrival, but the accident to the oil line decided him to have the cylinders reground and new pistons put in.

"We want to make the last lap a record," he said.

The delay was nerve-racking but it could not be helped. Tom was in communication with his father and Mary, and they, too, were eager for his success. All was well at home, Mary reported, and close guard was being kept on the Long Island hangar.

"They may try to blow us up when we make

our last landing," said Tom grimly, to his manager.

"They're equal to it," was Ned's answer. "What about Chicago and Denver?"

"I'm wiring the men there to be on the watch."

At last the overhauling of the *Osprey's* motor was finished, and after a test preparations for the trip back were made. Word that this was to be the final test of the airline express had been broadcast, and the papers all over the country were on the alert for news. It was almost like a presidential election.

In the half-light of a cold dawn Tom and his friends took the air from the San Francisco field. As they mounted upward Ned happened to glance at a calendar hanging on the wall of the car.

"Did you know that, Tom?" he asked.

"Know what?"

"That this is Friday the thirteenth?"

"Well, what of it?" asked the inventor.

"Don't you believe in luck?"

"Yes, when it's with me!" Tom said, with a chuckle. "Not otherwise. I saw a black cat as we were taking off, and I guess that will neutralize Friday the thirteenth. Don't worry!"

There seemed to be no cause for worry on the

first leg of the final trip. They got off very well, and under the care of Dolan, who had recovered from his indisposition, the *Osprey* winged her way across the mountains like the bird whose name she bore.

They were well ahead of their schedule when they landed in Denver, and luck was with them on the second lap, when Stone and his helper, with occasional relief from Tom and Ned, piloted the *Eagle* on its eastern journey.

"Well, Tom, old scout, it looks as if we were going to come through with flying colors!" cried Ned, as preparations to land in Chicago were being made.

"I hope so," was the answer.

There was a quick change of the car from the *Eagle* to the *Falcon* at the Chicago field, and Tom was about to give the signal to take off when a man with a reflex camera came dashing across the field. There had been a score of newspaper pictures taken, as well as many feet of movies, and Tom and Ned thought this man was a late-comer.

"Just a moment, Mr. Swift—please!" he cried, as he ran forward, his head almost inside the camera.

Tom was used to this plea from the hard-working newspaper picture-takers, and though he was anxious to be off he delayed a moment.

He knew it might mean the discharge of a man if he came back without a picture he had been ordered to get.

A reflex camera, as those interested in photography know, is one with a focal plane shutter, exceedingly rapid in action. It is much used in news photography. The operator raises a hood, which serves the same purpose as the black focusing cloth in the photograph gallery. To get sharp pictures it is necessary to focus up to the last moment. In the reflex camera the operator can see the image of the picture he is about to take on a ground glass. When the focal plane shutter is released this ground glass automatically drops out of the way.

Something in the actions of this man aroused the suspicions of Tom. He looked at him keenly for a moment as the fellow ran forward, his head almost inside his camera. Then, with a cry, Tom leaped out of the window of the car, and, like a football tackler, threw himself on the man. He knocked the fellow down, grabbed the camera and threw it as far as he could in a direction where there were no spectators.

"Look out!" yelled Tom. "It's a bomb!"

So it proved, for when the "camera" landed there was a sharp report and a puff of smoke, followed by a shower of dirt.

"I've got you, Schlump!" yelled the young inventor. Tom twisted the fellow's hands up on his own back as he rolled him over on his face and sat on the scoundrel.

Schlump it proved to be. He had hoped to get close enough not to be recognized by holding his face down in the fake camera. And he almost succeeded, adopting the guise of a newspaper photographer. The camera was but an empty black box with a fake lens. Inside Schlump held a bomb with a slight charge of powder in it. He dared not use much for he, himself, would be close when he hurled it.

But Tom had sensed the danger in time, and by his prompt action had saved himself and his friends from injury, if not death, and had saved the plane from damage.

"Hold him! I'll prefer charges against him after I reach New York!" cried Tom, as police officers hurried up and took the plotter in charge.

"You'll never get to New York!" boasted the prisoner.

But Tom did not let this threat worry him. Making a hurried explanation to the police captain in charge of the squad of officers, Tom saw the prisoner led away and then he took his place again.

"A narrow squeak, that," commented Ned.

"Just a little," admitted Tom, with a smile. "And now for the last lap."

The *Falcon* roared her way into the air amid the cheers of the throng, and the final stage of the journey was begun. At first it was feared lest some hidden defect might develop in the motor. But none did, the machinery working perfectly.

"They didn't get a chance this time," Tom decided. "And from the fact that Schlump tried so desperately at the last minute to disable us with a bomb, shows, I think, that they have fired their last shot."

But there was danger still in store for the daring aviator and his friends. They had made exceptionally good time from Chicago and were approaching the Long Island field. Tom was jubilant, for the record showed the best time yet made.

"There's the field!" cried Ned, from the after cockpit where he was helping manage the plane. Tom had decided, as was his right, to pilot the last stage of the journey himself.

"You're right!" admitted the young inventor as he gave a glance downward. "And there's a big crowd on hand to welcome us."

As they swung around into the wind, a puff of smoke was seen to arise from the hangar.

"Look at that!" cried Ned.

"Fire!" exclaimed Tom. "They may be trying to burn the place!"

Lower and lower the machine dropped, and those aboard could see the men in charge of the hangar making frantic signals for them not to drop too close to the big building. Tom heeded this advice, and swung down well away from the increasing volume of smoke. The *Falcon* came to a stop, and the young inventor and Ned climbed out of the cockpit.

"What's going on?" cried Ned to some of the workmen.

"Two masked men set the place on fire," was the answer. "But we've caught them, and the fire will soon be out. We were afraid you would come too close."

"Whew!" whistled Tom. "They're keeping up the fight until the last minute. So you caught the masked men, did you? Good! I'll have a look at them in a moment. But what's our time, Ned? We've completed our schedule and fulfilled our contract, but I'd like to know what actual running time we made this last trip in."

Ned did some rapid figuring. Then he uttered a cry of delight.

"What is it?" asked Tom.

"Fifteen hours and forty-six minutes!" was

the answer. "The best time ever made! You've broken all records, Tom!"

"I'm glad of it," was the modest reply.

"And so am I!" cried a voice, and Mary pressed her way through the milling throng to— well, what she did to Tom is none of your business nor mine, is it?

"Well, young man, you did what you said you would," came in the rasping voice of Jason Jacks. "Any time you want that hundred thousand dollars, or two hundred thousand, just let me know. I didn't believe much in this thing when you started, but you have proved that you can run an airline express between New York and San Francisco. There's a big future in it, I believe!"

"So do I," said Tom quietly. "And now I'd like to see who those masked men are."

When the men were brought before the young inventor and stripped of black face-coverings, they proved to be none other than Renwick Fawn and the man who variously called himself Blodgett and Barsky—the men who had endeavored to steal Tom's Chest of Secrets.

"I thought so!" said the young inventor. "So it was you who were back of this, with Kenny and Schlump. Well, we have both of them and now we have you."

"But I thought these two were in jail," said Ned wonderingly.

"They either escaped or bribed their way to a parole," returned Tom. "But they'll go back now."

And back went Fawn and Barsky to the prison from which, by means of political influence, they had been paroled. They had wanted revenge and had also tried, by corrupting Kenny and Schlump, to steal the airline express patents. But their plans had been frustrated.

"Did you really suspect, Tom, that the two masked plotters were Fawn and Barsky?" asked Ned.

"Not at first," was the answer. "Fawn has gotten over that queer trick of throwing out his elbow that surely would have given him away, and both men disguised their voices when they talked. They wanted to escape recognition, for they knew they might be sent back to jail on the old charges. Well, they'll do double time now—on the old charge, and for trying to kidnap me, as well as setting fire to the hangar."

"They played a desperate game," commented Ned. "To think of digging that tunnel and going to all that work to get your patents."

"They didn't dig the tunnel," Tom answered.

"It's a natural one. They just made an entrance to it near our fence—that much of the digging alone was new. The rest was natural. I may find a use for that same tunnel, too. It's a good thing to know about. And now, Ned, I'm going to take a little vacation."

"You deserve it!" answered the manager.

Thus the last of Tom's enemies were caught and sent away. Mr. Jacks was as good as his word, and not only invested largely in the new enterprise himself, but got his friends to do so, so that the money Ned and Mary had put in to bolster the sinking fortunes at the last minute was fully repaid them.

"I'd never have let you risk your savings, Ned, or you either, Mary, if I had known it," said Tom, when the story was told him. "Suppose I had failed?"

"Oh, I knew you wouldn't fail!" answered Ned.

"So did I," whispered Mary.

And that's that!

THE END

This Isn't All!

Would you like to know what became of the good friends you have made in this book?

Would you like to read other stories continuing their adventures and experiences, or other books quite as entertaining by the same author?

On the *reverse side* of the wrapper which comes with this book, you will find a wonderful list of stories which you can buy at the same store where you got this book.

Don't throw away the Wrapper

Use it as a handy catalog of the books you want some day to have. But in case you do mislay it, write to the Publishers for a complete catalog.

THE TOM SWIFT SERIES

By VICTOR APPLETON

Uniform Style of Binding. Individual Colored Wrappers.
Every Volume Complete in Itself.

Every boy possesses some form of inventive genius. Tom Swift is a bright, ingenious boy and his inventions and adventures make the most interesting kind of reading.

TOM SWIFT AND HIS MOTOR CYCLE
TOM SWIFT AND HIS MOTOR BOAT
TOM SWIFT AND HIS AIRSHIP
TOM SWIFT AND HIS SUBMARINE BOAT
TOM SWIFT AND HIS ELECTRIC RUNABOUT
TOM SWIFT AND HIS WIRELESS MESSAGE
TOM SWIFT AMONG THE DIAMOND MAKERS
TOM SWIFT IN THE CAVES OF ICE
TOM SWIFT AND HIS SKY RACER
TOM SWIFT AND HIS ELECTRIC RIFLE
TOM SWIFT IN THE CITY OF GOLD
TOM SWIFT AND HIS AIR GLIDER
TOM SWIFT IN CAPTIVITY
TOM SWIFT AND HIS WIZARD CAMERA
TOM SWIFT AND HIS GREAT SEARCHLIGHT
TOM SWIFT AND HIS GIANT CANNON
TOM SWIFT AND HIS PHOTO TELEPHONE
TOM SWIFT AND HIS AERIAL WARSHIP
TOM SWIFT AND HIS BIG TUNNEL
TOM SWIFT IN THE LAND OF WONDERS
TOM SWIFT AND HIS WAR TANK
TOM SWIFT AND HIS AIR SCOUT
TOM SWIFT AND HIS UNDERSEA SEARCH
TOM SWIFT AMONG THE FIRE FIGHTERS
TOM SWIFT AND HIS ELECTRIC LOCOMOTIVE
TOM SWIFT AND HIS FLYING BOAT
TOM SWIFT AND HIS GREAT OIL GUSHER
TOM SWIFT AND HIS CHEST OF SECRETS
TOM SWIFT AND HIS AIRLINE EXPRESS

GROSSET & DUNLAP,   PUBLISHERS,   NEW YORK

But Tom's *Osprey* had one advantage. Because of the heavy car slung below it, the center of gravity was thus made much lower than usual, and this served to keep the craft steady.

Tom glanced at the oil gage, at the gasoline indicator, and at the needle of the dial which showed their height above the ground. He had noted the tips of several jagged peaks below as they flew over them, and he realized that while they might be up sufficiently high in flying over level ground, they were not when traversing the Rocky Mountains.

"A little drop and we'll scrape some of those stone teeth," thought Tom. "I'm going up a bit."

He was in much more comfortable circumstances than had been the two men whom he and Ned relieved, for the storm garments protected him and his chum. Consequently Tom could give more undivided attention to managing the craft. His first act was to increase the speed of the motor and tilt the elevating rudder to send them higher.

"He's going to try to rise above the storm," decided Ned, though this was not actually Tom's idea. He merely wanted to be a little farther above those towering mountain peaks.

The *Osprey* responded well, and soon they had

CHAPTER XXII

KENNY BREAKS DOWN

THE quiet following the storm came as a great relief to Tom and Ned, alone up there in the cockpit of the plane. Though their friends were within a few feet of them, they really seemed quite isolated, for they could neither see nor hear the others in the car below them.

"Well, I'm glad we're out of that," remarked Tom, with a long breath—the first, seemingly, that he had taken in some time.

"Same here!" commented Ned. They were able to converse now by means of the speaking tube which connected the forward and aft cockpits, having only to overcome the roar of the motors and not the fierce rattle of the storm.

"And I guess if we do it inside of nineteen hours we've accomplished a lot," went on Tom. "The Broadway Limited thinks it's doing wonders if it goes from New York to Chicago in eighteen, but we have them skinned by several miles."

"You said it!" cried Ned, with justified en-